This is the story of how the deerslayers came to the Forest of Bealtuinn and of how a few people, angered by the slowness and apparent apathy of the authorities, decided to take the law into their own hands . . .

By the same author

FICTION

NOBLE PURPOSE

SUNSET IN THE EAST

THE DEVIL AND THE DEEP

THE LION AND FRANCIS CONWAY

THE DARK NIGHT

NON-FICTION

HOLIDAY FROM LIFE

PIGS I HAVE KNOWN

RED DUST OF AFRICA

THE DEERSLAYERS

by

SACHA CARNEGIE

LONDON : PETER DAVIES

FOR CHIQUITA,

WHEREVER SHE MAY BE

First published 1961

PRINTED AND BOUND IN GREAT BRITAIN FOR PETER DAVIES LTD.
BY HAZELL WATSON AND VINEY LTD., AYLESBURY AND SLOUGH

PROLOGUE

THE six red stags moving slowly from the good grass near the shore went warily as is their custom when travelling from place to place, well spaced like soldiers on patrol, and the only sound was the occasional flap of soft velvet ears. Five were young and of no great size, with the little twig horns of their youth, but the sixth was very big. Four feet high at the massive shoulders and with a black mane on him fit for a lion and the colour of his coat a deep chestnut brown. He carried his great head high and surveyed the scene about him with composure and dignity; his wet nose twitched slightly as he raised it to the morning breeze. He smelt nothing alien, no tainted scent of man came to him down the long Glen of the Skull. His large brown eyes were calm and untroubled.

The six of them moved among the black peat-pools and their tracks were deep in the soft black earth; as they went the young stags played among themselves, butting and prodding so that they got in his way, and he swept them from his path with a sudden sweep of his wide antlers. He was full of good rich grass, and soon he would sleep. But only when they reached the high ground far up on the rocky slopes of Creag Dhu, above the Cave of the Laughing Men.

A few hinds fed with their calves along the deep, twisting cleft of the Black Burn; the little deer ran to watch the otter inquisitively as he devoured his fish on a broad, white stone; they did not look up as their mothers did when the raven swooped low casting a skimming shadow across the tawny slope of Beinn Gobhair. The stag paid no heed to the hinds. In a month or so many would be his, but until then they held no fascination for him and he went on his way following his young companions up a path trodden by deer for countless years, along the bank of the Stag Burn, upwards, always upwards to safety.

There, a few hundred feet above the Cave of the Laughing Men, the stag lay down to rest with his back to a steep face of rock and heather. Not far away his special sentinel, a small beast not two years old, stood watchful, now and then tearing at the coarse brown grass, throwing up his head to sniff the warm air. Up there on the roof of the world he felt himself secure, tucked away beneath that overhang, looking down over the barren slopes of scree and thin heather to where sheep, those stupid useful lookouts, were browsing. At the first sign of men or dogs they would snort or run, and he would be warned. In the skies the ravens and the hooded crows would croak alarm at anything suspicious.

For the last three seasons he had spent the late summer and autumn on Creag Dhu, only descending to the low ground with the setting of the sun. Sometimes he did not bother to leave his sanctuary at all, but stayed to feed from the little grassy hollows and drink from the source of the Stag Burn. But September was the time of great danger when men were abroad on the hills and death struck suddenly and fast from nowhere. Not one of his other haunts was safe, and the autumn winds carried the disagreeable odour of man on their skirts.

This autumn was like no other, not unless you go back to the years of the great deer drives of two hundred-odd years ago. In those days the deer had fled before the shouting lines of beaters, the stench of black powder and the horrid reports of flintlocks; from the angry hum of musket balls flying from the rocks, the terrible sounds as the unlucky ones met death and wounds in the passes of Crionaig.

Certainly not since then had so many deer gathered in the Bealtuinn Forest. For the deer of the eastern mountains were moving towards the sea, driven from their own lands by the coming of men and vehicles in the darkness; by the sudden blinding terror of spotlights in which they were shot down, killed and maimed by stuttering guns which often left them to die in lingering agony. Calves and hinds and stags, it did not seem to matter; they all dropped to the heavy bullets or crawled away to die in the darkness with lead or splintered rock in their bellies.

Of course the stag did not know that. Nor did the stupid, useful sheep, nor any of the other animals lying hidden in the heather and the caves of Bealtuinn. But the ravens knew and the buzzards and the golden eagles that lived in the fastnesses of the Chasm: they knew, for they could fly far on their powerful wings; and with their keen eyes they could see the movement of the deer and knew there was meat in Crionaig.

And men knew. All sorts of men who began to turn their greedy, ruthless eyes towards the lonely, peaceful corner jutting like the prow of a great ship into the green Atlantic.

[1]

GAVIN BLAIR swung the wheel hard over and took the road for Glenaila. The lights of the old car were dimming and brightening, dimming again; by the sound of it, something was working itself loose in the engine. The front wheels jarred fiercely in a pothole. Two sheep turned their greenish glowing eyes towards him, then ran into the night; a few raggity clouds moved across the moon, promising wind but no rain. He needed rain; his grass needed more moisture than it got from the dew, for it was turning brown in the paddocks where the new rams were to go. The car was patently falling apart below him. He'd have to put it off the road for a day or so; if not, the poor old thing would pack up on him, and then he'd be really stuck. But not tomorrow, nor the next day either; probably not till the end of the week. He'd need at least four days to get the sheep off the hill, he was still so damned slow at the job. Gavin thought of his many little problems as he nursed the car slowly homewards.

Near Hump Bridge the lights failed completely, just as the moon went behind another cloud. He had to stop. With the moon he'd get home all right, lights or no lights. It wasn't as if he was on a populated road. No one came beyond the bridge, not unless they were visiting Glenaila. In fact, very few vehicles travelled on the roads of Bealtuinn at all, unless they had to. So it surprised him to see headlight beams approaching the bridge on the Fort Henry road. He watched the beams sweeping from side to side as the car negotiated the bends along the base of Sgurr Gheal, and he envied the driver the brightness of those lights. They lit the pale sheen of the mountain, then suddenly went out. The engine stopped and he could hear the small parched rustle of the river over the stones.

He thought he heard low voices; but could not be certain. They must surely be in trouble to stop like that in the middle of nowhere. He got out and walked towards the bridge. As he crossed the river his footsteps frightened some night bird which flew into the brightening moonlight with a sharp clatter of wings. This time he certainly heard a voice.

"What the hell was that?" it asked loudly.

"Shut up!"

Then a third voice rapped out: "Stand by."

Though they were much closer than he thought, Gavin could not make them out against the mountainside. There was a clink of metal.

"Now!"

The powerful spotlight cut through the pale darkness: a sudden silent blinding knifeblade. Gavin stopped in his tracks. The beam moved slightly to the right, and in it appeared the silver shapes of deer, motionless and pinned in a bunch to the hillside, heads up and eyes glinting like little embers.

"Let 'em have it!"

Flame stabbed from the muzzles of the weapons. An automatic sprayed a long burst down the spotlight beam and Gavin saw two animals leap in the air and go down. Someone was using a rifle; he could make out the rattle of the bolt, the thump and whine of the high velocity bullets. The deer huddled, not running, hardly moving except when they were hit, dazed and blinded, getting no wind of man, no sight of the bullets which struck them. The sub-machine gun swung farther right on to another group, chattering hysterically.

Then as quickly as it began the firing stopped and the mountains swallowed up the din as though it had never been. All that could be heard were the faint clatter of hooves on scree and the choking, coughing gasps as an animal drowned in its blood in the darkness.

"Come on, don't hang about. We'll load up the dead ones and what we can't put in the van we'll hide." The voice was educated and held authority. Gavin heard them put the weapons into their vehicle.

"Got the knife, Johnnie?"

"Aye."

"Well, come on then."

"I got two. I'm dead sure I got two." The man sounded very excited.

"All right, all right, don't wet yerself, Scrap."

Gavin moved very slowly along the edge of the road, stepping lightly on the grass; after a few steps he lay down and wormed forward on his stomach, peering at the sky where it met the crest of Sgurr Gheal. Soon he made out the shape of a small van silhouetted and a man standing by the back, his face towards the pinpoint torch bobbing on the lower slope. There was a sudden fierce struggle and the thump of hooves kicking at the ground.

"Quick, man, the knife."

Gavin inched closer to the van. The man lit a cigarette. He wore a cap and a high-necked sweater, and he whistled softly between his teeth. Presently the men returned, dragging a deer; they brought back five in all and hauled them into the back of the van.

"That's not bad," said one.

"Not bad? Not bad 'e says. Christ, boy, think yerself muckin' lucky we found 'em at all, first time out. 'Ow much for this little lot, guv?"

"Don't know, Scrap. Seventy pounds, if we're lucky."

"Seventy nicker! Christ, boy, we're sitting pretty. Money for muckin' old rope this is."

"There's another half-dozen that won't be getting far," put in the third man.

"Not with a gutful of slugs, eh, guv?"

"Shall we come back to look for 'em?"

"Let's get this lot home first. Better take her down to the bridge and turn." The engine started; the van bumped towards the bridge without lights.

"Got a fag, Johnnie boy?"

They lit their cigarettes and tossed away the matches. A match landed still burning in the grass some six feet from Gavin's face. Quite helpless he watched the flame take hold of the tinder grass and shoot up with a loud crackle.

"There's enough light without that bonfire."

A man stepped across to kick out the flames. Gavin pressed his face into the earth. Heavy boots stamped at the hard ground, then they paused and in the silence the man drew in his breath sharply.

"What the——?"

Gavin did as he had done in Korea when the Chinese had stumbled on him in the darkness: he leapt to his feet, yelling at the top of his voice, and went for the man with his head down and fists swinging. His knuckles smashed into flesh and bone; he drove his elbow into one stomach, his knee low into another, swiped back-handed at a gaping mouth and was through them racing for the bridge. Behind him he heard a confusion of shouts and curses and pounding boots; in front he heard the engine of the van coming back.

"Lights! Use your lights!" The man at the wheel was a quick thinker and he swerved the van at Gavin.

"Get him!"

Gavin saw the hump of the bridge looming close and jinked to his left, putting the van between himself and his pursuers. The bullet hit the parapet of the bridge with the slam of the shot and went whining into the night. He ducked at the sound and hurled himself off the road, rolling and scrabbling his way under the bridge. They'd look there, they'd be bound to, but where else was there, unless he ran for Creag Dhu, but they'd get the light on him before he was clear of the flats.

He lay in the shallows with the water flowing cold round

his body. They ran on to the bridge and at that moment the moon came out to show them the car; they made for it, all except one who peered into the darkness under the bridge. Gavin found a large stone and lay clutching it in his hand, waiting. But the man did not relish the vaulted darkness, not on his own, and he retreated to the road.

The others rejoined him and the four of them stood on the bridge. Gavin could not hear what they said for the noise of the water. He lay waiting for the torch beam or the spotlight to pick him out and then for them to come at him from both sides. He could expect short shrift, for he knew his blows had hurt, and one of them at least was prepared to shoot. But they did not come for him; they did not even look. They drove away.

He gave them a good half-hour before he emerged on the road. He was soaked and cold, his teeth chattered like castanets; his car had three flat tyres and the time was a quarter to two in the morning. He stood shivering in his sodden clothes, wondering what to do next. A bitter little wind came prowling along the Morie glen. One thing was certain: he could not stay there.

Heading back towards Rappoch he began to run.

* * * * *

"There's someone at the door, Donald." The policeman's wife shook her husband hard, for he was a sound sleeper; then she shouted right in his ear: "The door, Donald!"

He stirred sluggishly.

"Go on," she urged. "There is, I tell you."

He hunched himself deeper under the blankets. His wife heard the knocking on the door below.

"What would anyone be wanting at this unholy time of night?" he grunted angrily.

"If you go down to the door you'll maybe find out."

Constable McPhail, guardian of the law throughout the

land of Bealtuinn and in the twin parishes of Famista and Rappoch, struggled into his trousers and tunic.

"All right," he shouted angrily. "There's no need to be knocking the door down." His life was not normally packed with action, especially during the dark hours.

"Well?" He shone his torch on the figure at the door.

"May I come in?"

"Man alive, but it's Mr Blair. Come in, sir, come in." He bawled up the stairs for his wife to stir herself and make a pot of tea.

In the kitchen light Gavin was a forbidding sight. His smart suit was soaked and torn and smeared with mud; his shoes were squelching water and his black curly hair lay plastered to his skull; the knuckles of his right hand were badly skinned and blood trickled between the fingers. He sat on a chair while Donald poked the kitchen range into warmth and Mrs McPhail bustled about with kettles and teapots and basins.

Gavin drank the thick sweet tea as his clothes began to steam.

"Well, now, Mr Blair, and what's this all about?" Donald put on his best notebook voice.

"No, Donald, not yet. Wait while I get some dry things. Will you be showing me your hand, please, Mr Blair."

She hurried away. Gavin began to tell the policeman what had happened at the bridge. Half-way through, Mrs McPhail appeared with an old khaki shirt, a thick blue jersey and a pair of faded policeman's trousers.

"There you are, Mr Blair. I'm not saying they'll be fitting you, Donald's maybe a wee bit stouter here and there, but you'll be more comfortable. You'll be excusing me if I go back to bed for a wee while?" She left the kitchen, brushing aside Gavin's gratitude.

"And should we have been leaving you to stand and shiver on the doorstep?" asked the policeman.

Gavin finished his account. For a moment there was silence, broken by the purring note of the fire.

"And that will be all, Mr Blair?"

"Surely it's enough?"

"Aye, it's plenty, right enough," said the policeman slowly. "Mr Blair, you'll not have——" he began, then changed to: "You'll have been visiting?"

"Look, as I said, I had been over to Famista, having dinner with Captain Downie."

"Ah, yes, Captain Downie. A very hospitable man, I believe."

"If you mean, am I tight and imagining the whole damned thing, the answer's——"

"But, Mr Blair, you say they shot at you." Donald tapped the pencil against his teeth.

"I'll take you there in the morning and show you the bullet mark. Of course they shot at me. Look, one thing I do know and that's the noise of a bullet."

Donald opened the table drawer and got out paper, pen and a bottle of ink.

"Right, sir. Now it's facts I'll be wanting."

Gavin told the whole story again, very slowly to keep pace with the maddening scratch of the pen.

"A van, you say?"

"That's right."

The nib spluttered and scratched.

"And how many men were you saying?"

"Four, anyway."

"Hm-mm—four a-n-y-w-a-y." He blotted. "That's it so far. Now, Mr Blair, you're sure they were using an automatic weapon?"

"Absolutely, yes."

Donald's broad, flat face puckered all over with concentration as he wrote the word automatic.

"And you were saying there was a Cockney speaking among them?"

"That's what he sounded, yes."

"I am remembering a Cockney we had as sergeant-major in the war, a very diligent man at his work."

Gavin clenched his fists under the table. He was tired and irritable, and nothing was being done as far as he could see of any use whatsoever.

"Look, constable, couldn't you telephone to Fort Henry?"

"No, sir, we'll not be telephoning, not from here. The line is out of order, and that is the third time in a month. Sometimes I'm wondering what they are using the wires for, Mr Blair. But in the morning I shall be going to make my report. Now, what time was it you were leaving Famista House?"

The inquiry dragged on. Mrs McPhail reappeared, dressed. She let in the morning sun. Gavin yawned and stared out of the window with prickling eyes. The early sunlight lay along the side of a little hill; sheep were grazing on the slope and hens scratched among the little conical piles of hay. It was sleepy and warm and supremely lazy. Nothing would stir these people, he thought ruefully. Nothing less than an explosive charge. With an effort he pulled himself together.

"What are we going to do then?"

"Well, Mr Blair, the best thing you could be doing is to be going home and get some sleep. I am thinking I should go down to Kenny Carmichael and get him to drive us to Sgurr Gheal and let us see with our own eyes what you have been telling me. Lizzie, tell Calum I'm needing a word with him. Can we be managing another for breakfast? You'll be staying and taking a bite with us, Mr Blair?"

A small freckled boy came running in, rubbing the sleep from his eyes.

"Calum," said his father, "you'll go at once to Kenny and ask him to come here with his van. On a matter of urgency you'll tell him, and I'll be obliged if he could be coming at once."

"Aye, dad, and if Kenny's not in, what shall I do then?"

"You'll go to the Manse and give the same message to the Minister. Is that clear, Calum?"

"Yes, dad." He scampered away.

Donald moved from the room more slowly. Gavin sat and talked to Mrs McPhail as she turned the spitting sausages in the pan. He realised how exhausted he was, how hungry, and how very kind these people were. The innate courtesy of the Gael, he thought wryly, glancing at the clock and wondering where the van had got to with its load of butchered deer and men who were prepared to shoot if anyone got in their way. A fat white cat rubbed itself against his leg and hens peered through the half-open door, heads on one side, murmuring confidentially.

He wondered what Margaret would say.

[2]

THEY stood by the dying calf, the three of them: Gavin, the policeman and Kenny Carmichael, the owner of the Rappoch store, postmaster and lord knows what else. He had about him the look of a Norseman, with his flaxen hair and the pale blue eyes that blazed with anger as they looked on what the poachers had done. His strong hands clenched and unclenched and he swore steadily under his breath.

"Poor wee thing," said Donald. "Can we not be putting it out of its misery?" Gavin ran to his car for the starting-handle. The calf was hideously wounded, shot through the hindquarters by heavy bullets; it had tried desperately to drag itself over the rocks, but the front legs had not the strength and now it lay panting with lolling tongue and rolling terrified eyes. Not far away lay a hind which might have been the mother, shot to bits about the belly.

Gavin brought down the handle with all his strength on the back of the head where it joined the soft fur of the neck. The little animal jerked convulsively. the front legs thrashed and dark blood flooded from the mouth. Closing his eyes, he struck again, and again till Donald put a restraining hand on his upraised arm.

"It's dead, Mr Blair," he said quietly. "It'll not be needing any more."

Gavin dropped the handle and sat down on a rock, hit hard by fatigue and anger. He was shaking slightly.

"It must have been like that for five hours."

"The bastards," said Kenny. "The murdering bastards."

"Now do you believe me?"

"Aye, Mr Blair. I am believing you right enough."

Hooded crows circled the peak of Sgurr Gheal, and their

sinister shadows moved across the hillside, this way and that. Gavin watched the birds, remembering a story John Grant the stalker, had once told him. ". . . and there was the lamb I'm telling you, half-born, not yet free of the mother and a hoodie going for one of its eyes. Man alive, but they're filthy devils. . . ." An immediate introduction to the cruelty of the world.

Flies were gathering on the calf's battered little head. But at least it had been spared the horror of the hoodies and the black-backed gulls. And after them the ravens to disembowel the still living animals with merciless beaks.

They searched the area and found three more beasts: two dead hinds and a young stag trying to die, with all four legs smashed at the knees and a bullet through the lower jaw. There was blood streaked black on the rocks, and rusty tracks where the carcases had been dragged across the grass. Many of the boulders were chipped and splintered. Kenny brought the starting-handle. It did not take the stag long to die.

"God knows how many more of the poor brutes have crawled away to die," said Gavin bitterly.

"Ach," spat Kenny, "this is something that sickens you and makes you want to kill."

"I'll tell John Grant. He'll look for them."

There was nothing more they could do. Gavin took the policeman and showed him the bullet mark on the bridge. Donald shook his head silently. Men who were willing to shoot to save themselves; this was something new.

Not that there hadn't been poaching of the deer now and then, but the work of men who picked their beast and shot carefully to kill. Many's the late evening and early morning he had been out with John Grant to watch for the poacher lads. Sometimes they caught their men, more often not. Usually they went chasing over the hills after the shot and found no more than the head and innards of the beast. But this . . .

"This is nothing but——" He searched for the right word to describe this shambles.

"Murder. Filthy, bloodstained murder."

"Aye, Mr Blair, and it could have been worse. It could have been yourself lying there with them."

He wrote in his notebook. Gavin walked up the road to where the match had burnt. The charred patch was there, beside the road. It had certainly all happened.

"Heh! Over here. Look." Kenny had wandered back to the scene of the massacre. They joined him. He stood above a calf that crouched at his feet, too terrified to move.

"It's not touched."

"Maybe it's stunned," said Donald.

They looked at the little shivering thing. Its coat was softly spotted with white and its small muzzle was of grey velvet like its ears; the wide-open eyes were the dark brown of liquid honey. It was panting quickly. Gavin stooped towards the little animal, and as it felt his fingers it screamed, just like a frightened child, and quivered violently beneath his touch.

"Will we have to kill it?" Kenny asked slowly.

"Aye," said Donald. "The poor wee beast'll still be on its mother and likely she's lying somewhere hereabouts or gone away to die."

"Well, I'm not killing it," said Kenny flatly.

Gavin picked up the calf and held it, bleating and feebly struggling, in his arms.

"There's not going to be any more killing. I'm taking it home to Glenaila. My wife'll be delighted, she's always wanted something like this. We'll try and bring it up on a bottle, then when it's big enough it can go back to the hill."

"I doubt it'll not be leaving you, Mr Blair. They never do, not when you bring them up."

"Well, then it'll become part of the farm." He stroked between the ears, and soothed with gentle words.

"There, it's all right. You're safe now. I'll take you home and put you in a safe warm place and you'll be all right." His voice and touch seemed to comfort the calf, for it lay more quietly in his arms and ceased to struggle so violently. They put it in the back of Kenny's van, where it lay on sacking with its heart beating like a small sledgehammer. They took it to Glenaila and laid it in clean straw in the byre. By the time Gavin had fed it from a lambing bottle and they had all patted it and said encouraging things, the calf was on its feet and no longer showing signs of fear. They left it investigating the cobbled stones of the byre and snuffling at the walls.

"In a couple of days it'll be following you everywhere," said Kenny. "What will you be calling the little creature?"

Gavin laughed. "Better leave that to my wife, I think."

"Bambi," suggested Donald without much originality.

"Ach, no, Donald. It needs a tougher name than that."

They reached the bridge.

"I'll be telling Murdo Finlay to come out and put your car in order, Mr Blair."

"Thanks, Kenny. No, I think I'll just stay here till he comes."

"Don't you be worrying yourself. They'll not be getting away with this. We'll be getting them, if we have to go after them ourselves." The Viking eyes blazed into quick anger. "I'd not be minding a go at them." He regarded his large fist.

"Now, Kenny, the law will be taking care of this," corrected Constable McPhail rather pompously. Kenny said nothing but winked at Gavin as he got into his van. Gavin lay down on the warm grass and tried to relax. The river trickled over the stones; he heard distant sheep and thought of how much he had to do on the farm. A curlew filled the sky with the liquid magic of its call, and one raven answered another as they both spied death on the golden slope of the mountain.

He opened his eyes and watched a dipper bobbing on a

stone; the water lapped its feet as it jerked up and down like a fat, bowing waiter. The clouds last night had promised wind, but no wind had come. Instead, the sultry heat of another peerless day and all the beauty in the world around him. The scavenging birds croaked above the dead shapes of deer stiffening in the sun. He could see the pale blob of a hind lying up there. He closed his eyes.

So now they had come to Bealtuinn. Poaching gangs had been operating inland for years now, ever since the war when meat was hard to come by and no one asked many questions. In some areas deer poaching had become almost part of the scenery. Why not, when the penalties were so pitifully inadequate? They spoke of some new Act or other which would allow stiffer sentences. It might help, but he had his doubts. No one seemed to care much. But the stalkers cared: they cared a great deal, and many of the police did too. But the courts so often let them down and the poachers walked out laughing, planning their next coup. And now they were here with their murdering guns. What would happen now? Constable McPhail would make his report to superiors in Fort Henry; investigations would be set in train, questions asked. Other policemen would probably come to Bealtuinn. He might have to go into Fort Henry himself. So long as they kept it out of the papers, or there'd be a crowd of nosey-parker reporters poking round Glenaila, wasting time and wanting to see the Bridge of Death. Gavin smiled slightly. He wished Margaret was with him. He always felt so damnably alone without his wife. They had been married for eighteen months and he loved her very dearly; her head, as well as being remarkably pretty, contained a great deal of good sense and she would have many ideas—she always did—about everything under the sun. He smiled again. Still, only another couple of days and she'd be back with him and life's little problems would be that much easier to face.

He grew very drowsy in the murmuring warmth and fell deeply asleep till Murdo arrived to sort the car.

* * * * *

The wind of the killing had sent the deer running through the moonlight, jostling and bumping in their frantic efforts to escape. And even with the coming of dawn they did not settle but kept on the move in sudden scary rushes; perhaps a hundred yards, perhaps half a mile. Small groups huddled, scattered wildly, huddled close again, and the hinds would lower their heads to the grass. The slightest thing—the movement of a sheep, the cry of a raven, a curlew taking wing—up went every twitching nose into the whispering breeze.

Nor were the stags any calmer. The big black fellow stood watchful and ready for flight, every sense strung taut by the presence of danger. He felt that something in the air which tells an animal to be alert and ready for instant flight. The whispering breeze eddied mischievously and swept the smell of man up to where he stood. With a snort the big stag turned and ran, holding his head high, moving very silently for so large a beast, away over the summit of Creag Dhu and down into the little glen of the Stag Burn.

John Grant was searching for wounded deer. The stalker was a very big man; over six foot three and with a breadth to match. In his youth he had been a man to turn the head of any woman born, and even now in his sixty-ninth year he was an impressive figure with his great frame, his heavy grizzled beard, deep-set blue eyes a little faded by the years, and the slow, lilting speech of his race.

If he did not carry himself so straight you could blame the lump of German steel received in his back at Ypres. For the last few years the wound had been slowly crippling him; that and the stiffness of age gripping at his hands and legs. And now this bloody arthritis in the knee. He sat for a moment to get his wind back after the climb from the road. This would be his last year on the hill. He did not need a doctor to tell him that. And without the hill he would be lost and utterly miserable. For it had been his life since he had been old enough to hold a glass steady to his eye and watch the red deer on Beinn Gobhair behind his father's house.

Murdo Grant had been head stalker on the Forest of Bealtuinn, and his father before him. Except for five years in the army it was the only life that John Grant had known: living and working among the deer. In his own way he loved them, and because he loved his deer he always swore the only man fit to kill them—other than himself—was one who knew how to handle a rifle, how to stalk over the hardest country and how to kill cleanly and instantaneously.

Since young Sir George had left his home for Canada there had been few men who could measure up to Grant's standards. It had sickened him to see the syndicates that came to Bealtuinn. Perhaps it would not be a bad thing to leave the Forest, aye, and let the Lodge fall to ruin so that none would come there any more; only the ravens and the buzzards and the deer. He sat brooding for a while, filled with the deep dark melancholy of his people, then he got slowly to his feet; cursing the pain of his knee. There would likely be more wounded beasts to be finished off.

He had already found two hinds and shot them near the road by Piper's Croft. Now he crossed the river and climbed into the area of hillocks and hollows on the southern slopes of Sgurr Gheal. On his bearded face was a thin little wind from the north east bringing with it the first suggestion of winter.

A young hind lay in one of the hollows, and the moss on which she lay sucked the blood from her punctured stomach and from the ragged hole behind the shoulder. Two bullets had torn through her belly, large copper bullets which smashed and pulped and brought terrible pain in their wake.

A splinter of rock had ripped into her lungs so that she breathed a pinkish bubbly froth.

At first she had run on wobbling legs from the terror of the light, but the wounds were soon too much for her courage and she had sunk down in the hollow where she lay for many hours waiting to die and not understanding. Other deer came close but shied away from the blood, and the only living thing that visited her was a big dog fox; which sat on its haunches to watch and to wait.

The poor beast closed her eyes, hoping to escape the awful fire in her guts, and her head sank lower as her life dribbled into the soft yellow moss. The breath gurgled loosely in her throat; once or twice she tried to lick away the pain, but had not the strength. When the sun cleared the mountains it found the hind still alive; it struck warm in the eyeless sockets and on the hooded crows as they squabbled over the terrible delicacies.

And that was how the stalker found her. He ended her suffering with a bullet in the head.

"Poor beastie," he said aloud, slamming home another round. He stood by the mutilated body and cursed as Kenny had done, long and fluently, in his own tongue. The fox loped out of sight, red-bright in the morning light; the ugly birds sat gorged but hoping for more.

For a while John Grant spied the likely places where he knew he might find wounded animals. It did not take long to spot another lying in the shadow of a knoll just above the Black Burn. He whistled to his dog and went as fast as his leg would allow.

That was four, but there would be more of them, wandering dazed and bleeding through the Forest of Bealtuinn.

* * * * *

Whenever Constable McPhail visited Fort Henry to make a report he had to deal with his immediate superior, Sergeant

Georgison, which was very convenient and pleasant, the two of them being brothers-in-law and getting on so well together. The sergeant was married to the constable's sister, Jeanie; they had fought a good deal of the war in the same battalion and had many memories in common.

But on this day Sergeant Georgison was buttoned up and unsmiling; this was no social meeting. He was a slow-moving heavy man, dark of countenance, fleshy round the jaw and always giving the impression that his collar was a size too tight. His eyes were narrowed by a frown of irritation as he read through Donald's report. At length he sat back, jabbing at the paper with his pencil.

"And what," he inquired gloomily, "can I be doing with this?"

"Well, now, Davie, you could be——" No, it was not the day for the making of jokes.

"You'll have been hearing of such a thing as proof?"

"Aye, Sergeant, but it'll not be easy come by."

"There's the bullet hole, right enough, and the deer lying dead all over the place and this—this statement you were taking from Mr Blair. I know you've put it all down, Donald. But it's not enough, not for Himself in there." The sergeant nodded at the door. "What can I be saying to him?" He consulted the report. "A van. Might be blue, might be black. No number. Four men. Might have been five. One of them called 'Scrap', another one Johnnie. A tommy gun. How does he know it was a tommy gun?"

"Would you not be knowing the sound of a tommy gun yourself? The man was in the army, Davie. Aye, he'll be knowing such things."

Georgison got up and made for the window, where he stood staring out at various nondescript inhabitants of Fort Henry.

"All we can be doing," said Donald, "is to wait and hope they'll be trying again. I'll be keeping my ears open and when

I'm hearing anything, anything at all, I'll be letting you know."

"You and your bicycle." Georgison snorted, but not unkindly. "Man, but you should be having a car. To catch these fellows you need to be on the move, Donald. They'll not be waiting for you to come up with them on your bicycle." A bell shrilled, angrily.

"Himself's in the tearing hurry he's always in." The sergeant vanished next door with the report.

Inspector Marr was not a local man. He came from a part of the country where, in his own view, things were done with very much more speed and decision. He was a stout balding man with a brusque manner and a great kindness of heart.

"Now look here, Georgison, what about this business of these blasted parking notices?"

"It's done," retorted the sergeant curtly.

"Oh, it's done, is it? Don't bother to let me know, I only sit at this desk as a blasted ornament, just for the fun of it. Well, what's that you've got there?" The sergeant placed the report in front of the Inspector without a word. He watched the expression change as Marr read the words.

"D'you think this is true?"

"Yessir."

The Inspector leant back in his chair, pulling thoughtfully at his pugnacious little moustache. "God's sakes, Georgison, I'd hoped we'd not be bothered by these blasted poachers, and in McPhail's area too."

"Constable McPhail's a good man, sir."

"I know he's a good man. But no one could call him the world's fastest mover. Look here, I've talked to people who've had dealings with deer poachers. You know as well as I do, Georgison, it's no earthly use bringing a poacher to court unless you've caught him—like that, bang in the act, with a round up the spout and the dead beast still warm. Otherwise it's a waste of time. And what's more," he added angrily, "it makes us a bloody laughing-stock. Proper Charlies, we look." Inspector Marr glanced down at the report.

"This man, Blair, know anything about him?"

"He farms sheep and a few cattle. A place on the sea. Glenaila. Lives there with his wife, so Constable McPhail was telling me."

"Reliable witness?"

"An ex-officer."

"I see."

Inspector Marr was also an ex-officer. There was a short pause.

"A man not easily scared, or so Donald—Constable McPhail—was telling me."

"Scared? Why should he be scared?"

"You'll have heard of the man who lost his stackyard because he reported a gang of these poachers. There've been other cases too, Inspector, of people not willing to say what they knew."

"Think they might try it on him?"

"Well, sir, if they shot at him once they might be doing it again. He was upsetting their little game and hitting them. They'll not be liking that. Will they, now?"

"Not much, no. But I rather wonder if they'll come back. After all, Georgison, there must be plenty of other quieter places where men don't suddenly appear out of the night and hit them in the face."

"Constable McPhail was having a word with John Grant—he is the stalker at Bealtuinn Lodge—and he was saying they would be back."

"What makes him so sure?"

"He was saying there have never been so many deer in the Forest as at the moment. He says that when the snow comes and drives the deer to the low ground, then these poachers will be back."

"I see. Who lives at this Bealtuinn Lodge?" Inspector Marr

had not been at Fort Henry for very long and was not familiar with every corner of his large beat.

"Nobody. The place is empty all the year except for the stalking. It is a syndicate that comes up for the stalking. This year they are not coming. I believe the Lodge will be empty."

"So Grant would be free to do a bit of watching?"

"He will not be minding that at all, Inspector. He is not a man to be standing nonsense from poachers, nor from anyone else. Aye, John Grant is an excellent man to have on our side."

Marr jotted names on a slip of paper. "Blair. Grant. McPhail. Who else is there in that area? Who could be relied upon to help, I mean?"

"Well now——" Sergeant Georgison stared at the ceiling for so long that Marr thought his neck had stuck. These Highlanders. If they could find an excuse for dawdling . . .

"Well, there is Kenny Carmichael, he is a tidy enough shot with a rifle, and then——"

"God sake's, man, we're not recruiting an army of snipers!"

". . . then there is Captain Downie, living at Famista. A Commando or some such during the war, and a man about the size of John Grant. I'm thinking there are some good men in Bealtuinn."

The Inspector added the two names. "Better tell McPhail to play the thing down as much as he can."

"I was telling him that myself."

"Excellent, Sergeant, excellent. You'll finish at the Yard yet. We don't want the place cluttered up with newspapermen. By crackers, if they got wind of someone being shot at —the place'd be crawling with 'em." He laughed. "Think of the headlines, Georgison, think of the headlines. Sheep Farmer Foils Desperate Gang. Flirting With Death In The Highlands." He rummaged in his tray.

"Get through to Inverness with all the dope you've got. The van. Precious little there." With his other hand he flipped through the report. "Johnnie. Scrap. Might be a help." He found his cane beneath a pile of paper. "I'm due in court in ten minutes. Yes, we don't want the whole of Scotland to know about this. God knows, all the Bealtuinn people will be chattering their silly heads off and everyone saying why can't anything be done, why are the police sitting on their great fat arses taking it easy while the poachers run rings round 'em. Between you and me and that empty inkpot there's precious little we can do at the moment except to make the usual routine inquiries and wait. Sooner or later we'll get the buzz whether they're local men or not." He jammed his cap on his head and made for the door.

"Tommy guns! Rifles! And not one of the bloody things licensed, I'll bet." He vanished at his usual brisk pace, only to come darting back.

"Put Farquhar on to the butchers and game dealers." He was away. He was back.

"Don't press the inquiries, Sergeant. Not at this stage. Keep 'em casual. I want the impression to get about that we couldn't care less if the deer are slaughtered in their bloody hundreds." He was away for the third time. Sergeant Georgison sighed heavily. The hustle and bustle of the fellow! But he had a good head on him, right enough. He went next door to pass on the Inspector's remarks.

That night, as he lay awake beside his plump, pretty little wife, Sergeant Georgison suddenly began to see a pleasant vision unfolding across the darkness: that of himself being acclaimed as the man who really broke the poaching gangs in Scotland. Flattering phrases addressed to himself dripped from the lips of senior officers. Flamboyant headlines strung themselves across the night; pictures of Sergeant Georgison, full-face, in profile; smiling and grim. Ambition was stirring. In a sudden access of enthusiasm he reached for his small, plump wife.

[3]

NEXT morning when Kenny was sweeping out his little store-cum-post office, long before any of his normal customers were expected, a car drew up and the Blairs appeared in the shop. Kenny leaned on his broom.

"It's good to see you back, Mrs Blair."

"Not half as wonderful as it is to be home," Margaret smiled.

"What can I do for you?" He retired behind the counter and became business-like.

"Bacon, sugar, butter, bread—oh, everything." She glanced fondly at her husband. "I'm sure he's been living on air since I went away."

Her eyes were long and grey, her nose short, her mouth a little too big for the smallness of her face. Not that it mattered, Kenny thought, pouring sugar. It did, in fact, add very considerably to her attraction. Margaret Blair was twenty-eight, some seven years younger than her husband, and, on a miniature scale, a most attractive woman. Kenny weighed the sugar, thinking, she could sit on the palm of my hand, and smiled to himself at the idea.

"Will that be all?" he asked her.

"Don't rush me, Kenny."

He could not take his eyes from the trim little figure in the grey coat and skirt; the dark curls under the scarlet beret, the extraordinary whiteness of her neck. The wide mouth opened in another smile as her eyes met her husband's. She laughed and chattered nineteen to the dozen, examining things, asking Gavin for his advice. Aye, it was good to see people so happy.

"Has he been buying any *proper* food at all?"

"Of course I have. Why, I've been in here every day spending a small fortune on my stomach. Isn't that so, Kenny?"

"I only hope you've remembered to bury all the tins."

"Any sign of that fencing stuff yet?" Gavin asked.

"No, not yet, Mr Blair. The carrier hasn't been since last Thursday."

"Damn!"

"Now, don't be upsetting yourself. I'm thinking maybe he'll be calling sometime tomorrow. Aye, it should be tomorrow right enough."

"Tomorrow! It's always tomorrow."

"That's what's so wonderful, darling."

"Yes, I know, that's all very well, but how do we keep the new rams penned without wire?" The doorbell tinkled.

"A difficult problem, Mr Blair, a difficult problem."

The Minister stepped into the shop on his rubber soles, in his silent bouncy way, smiling and nodding affably all round.

The Reverend Andrew Sinclair was in his forty-fifth year but did not look it, for his face was surprisingly unmarked for someone who had gone through the sorrow of losing a dearly loved wife two years before. Now he lived alone in the small grey Manse above the kirkyard. Alone, that is, except for a crotchety old person, a sort of cook-cum-housekeeper called Mrs Macleod who what they called 'did' for him. Now and then his daughter, who was studying at Aberdeen University, came home to visit her lonely father. He was a most likeable man, the Minister, much respected by the great majority of his widely scattered and sparsely populated parish. For he was an energetic and conscientious flock-master who worked himself unsparingly in the service of the poor and the needy.

There may perhaps have been a few of the older folk who considered his preaching of religion to approach on occasions a bit too close to what they thought of as 'free-thinking', for unlike many of his fellows the Reverend Sinclair did not hold religion above their heads as a scourge and a constant threat of eternal damnation and all the rest of it, but rather as something to help and encourage. He was no hell-fire and brimstone man.

Gavin and Margaret got on very well with him. Often a long winter evening would be enlivened by the Minister and his chessboard, or his draughtboard (chess with Gavin, draughts with Margaret), or just his fund of interesting and amusing anecdotes.

"There's hope for the Church yet, with men like that working for it." That was Mike Downie's view on the Minister.

Now, seeing Margaret, he removed his pale tweed hat from his head and the pipe from his firm, generous mouth. He made his customary short bow.

"Ah, Mrs Blair, I am delighted to welcome you back. And how was the great city of London?"

"Much the same as usual, everyone pushing and shoving and hurrying at top speed and treading very hard on everyone else's toes. I wasn't sorry to leave it."

"No, indeed. Life down there could almost be on a different planet. A quarter of the usual, please, Kenny. Yet even this little community of ours is no longer so peaceful." He turned to Gavin. "I trust you're recovered from your unpleasant experience of the other night?"

"Yes, thanks," said Gavin, not looking at his wife. He had not told her; why worry her at once. He had been going to show her the calf and then tell her the whole story.

"Splendid, splendid. A shocking incident by all accounts. Your husband is a very fortunate man, Mrs Blair, very fortunate indeed."

"Yes, isn't he?" she said lightly.

"Please forgive me, Mr Blair, if I am being inquisitive, but did one of these scoundrels actually shoot at you?"

"Aye, Minister," blurted Kenny. "And haven't I seen the bullet mark with my own two eyes?"

Margaret's eyes were dark grey saucers.

"Good heavens, did they hit you?" exclaimed the Minister.

"No. Only the bridge."

"Ah, I see."

"They're a wicked lot, Mrs Blair," put in Kenny. "It is best not to be thinking of them."

"Yes," she murmured, "aren't they?"

The Minister relit his pipe. "But is anything being done?" he asked through the smoke.

"It's in the hands of the police."

"Constable McPhail?"

"Among others."

"Ah, I see." The pipe sputtered wetly in the short silence.

"These poacher fellows should not be getting away with it so easily this time." Kenny poured the Minister's bull's-eyes on to the scales with a loud clatter. "They say," he went on with mounting indignation, "the sheriffs do nothing but wag their fingers at these boys and then let them off with a silly wee fine. That's not right at all. It's inside they should be going. But what else can we be expecting with things as they are, run from London or one of they places?" The Norseman eyes swept over them angrily. He rammed the top on the jar. "Give us more say in our own affairs and we'd soon be putting a stop to this poaching lark." He snorted. "What do they folk in their dainty white collars know about the deer? And they don't care. I'm telling you, they don't care. Indeed, I'm thinking it pays some of them not to be caring," he finished darkly.

"Come now, Kenny, you'll not be blaming every shower of rain on the wicked men of Whitehall." The Reverend Andrew Sinclair smiled his pleasant smile.

Kenny regarded him thoughtfully. "No, Minister, I'll not be doing that, but"—he paused—"but—well, something's got to be done."

"I am sure the police will take all the steps necessary to

catch these people, should they try to come back to Bealtuinn."

"Maybe, Minister, maybe," said Kenny doubtfully. He shoved the Minister's bag of sweeties across the counter and turned to Gavin.

"If it's help you're needing, Mr Blair, just call for me. Sometimes it gets a wee bit dull in here, I'm telling you." He grinned, brightening considerably at the thought of action. "I'm not too bad with a rifle myself."

"There cannot be a man in the parish who doesn't consider himself handy with some form of firearm or other." The Reverend Sinclair took possession of his bull's-eyes. There were many rifles scattered among the villages and crofts of Bealtuinn; everyone knew that. Mostly service rifles of a certain age which had found their way back from the wars. In the old days weapons had been concealed in the thatch or buried in the ground, now they lay in the attics, in the byres or sometimes beneath a floorboard. Few, if any, were legally recognised, and most of them had a good supply of Government ammunition.

On still days Gavin often heard the shooting on the shore near Famista as bottles were shattered in the Bay of the Many Waves. Now and then Constable McPhail would mount his bicycle and pedal slowly towards the sound of the guns; but as he could be seen approaching all the way from the Bridge of the Axe, he never found anything more than some fishermen with bland faces throwing stones at the bobbing bottles and tins.

Some of these rifles were used in the evenings or just as dawn broke, when the deer were feeding close to the shore; quite a number of families fed royally on venison. Everyone knew that too. John Grant was on good terms with many of the culprits, but he was not a man to meet on a dark night, not if you'd been after his deer. But that sort of poaching was an integral part of life, always had been; like the roar of the sea or the soft grey wind that came from the Atlantic.

"You could put a fully armed platoon in the field from Rappoch alone."

"Aye, Mr Blair, I'm thinking you're not far wrong there." Kenny let out a great bellow of laughter.

"It sounds as though——" began the Minister, but Kenny was away, the bit firmly between his teeth.

"A wee bullet in their tyres and they'd not be so keen on meddling with the Bealtuinn deer. Aye, or a few broken heads among them and they'd be looking for a quieter part of the country to do their murdering in."

"But, Kenny, that would be war," said the Minister, twinkling perceptibly.

"Aye, Minister, so it would. But a lot of folk are saying something should be done to stop these gangs, aye, something that will be shaking them properly."

"Well, let us hope——" But what he hoped was never made clear, for, clutching his bag of bull's-eyes, the Reverend Sinclair raised his hat to Margaret, nodded at Gavin and left the shop in his silent, bouncy way. There was a silence.

"Don't be minding me, Mrs Blair, I'm always shouting my head off. But," he added to Gavin, "remember, if you're ever needing help, you know where to come."

"I won't forget, Kenny."

"Now we must be going home," said Margaret, speaking for the first time. "There'll be lots to do, and I'm sure you've got lots to tell me. *Haven't* you, darling?"

Kenny carried out the box of stores. "If I'm hearing anything, Mr Blair, I'll be letting you know."

Margaret did not speak till they had turned on to the Glenaila road. "Now, love-of-my-life, would it be too much to ask what on earth all that was about?"

Gavin stopped at Hump Bridge, switched off the engine, thought for a while and then told her. He told her everything except how they had found the wounded deer, for, like him, she really loved animals. What he did tell her upset her enough, as he knew it would. When he had finished she sat in silence for a long moment, staring at the shining mass of Sgurr Gheal.

"Oh, Gavin, no. Not here. Not in Bealtuinn."

He put his arm round her shoulders; she relaxed against him with her head on his shoulder. "Yes, darling, I'm afraid they are here. With a vengeance." He held her closer. "I wish to hell I hadn't had to tell you this, first thing after you're back."

"I'm still pleased to be home." She lifted her face to his, and he kissed her.

"I love you, Margaret. You know that, don't you?"

"Yes, my dearest, I know. And I love *you*. Very, very much." He kissed her again.

"But what *is* to be done?" she asked, as they drove home.

"God knows! But something, anyway, that's certain. I think we'd better have a talk to Mike and see what he thinks, and John, of course. Between us we ought to work out some way of catching these brutes if they come back."

"Will they?"

"I think very likely, yes."

There was a diver splashing on the surface of the Wailing Loch; Gavin slowed to watch it, then drove on round the shoulder of the Big Sister.

"Home," cried Margaret. "Oh, darling, you've painted the windows."

"Like them?"

"Like them! They're lovely."

He went very slowly for the last hundred yards; he always did. For he enjoyed the sight of their house, white against the greeny background of the sea. Glenaila was a square, two-storeyed farmhouse with attendant byres and outhouses; it was roofed with old slates and roughly harled, under a coat of whitewash. When they had first come round the Big Sister and seen it through the drizzling rain, the house had looked forlorn, uncared-for and depressing beyond words; most of the windows were broken and large patches of harling were crumbling from the damp insidious touch of the sea winds; quite a number of slates lay smashed in the long grass. The dreary sigh of the wind through the empty place had almost sent them running, their tails between their legs, back to civilisation.

But now it stood bright and sturdy and welcoming in the sunlight; the newly painted windows gleaming red. Margaret looked at their home, at the sea sweeping in beyond the rough sea-meadow and their little pier; at the neat, well-mown square of lawn and the strip of rolled grass round the base of the house, the three small flower-beds with their stumpy roses. He had even found time to rake the gravel and polish the brass angel head on the red door, specially for her return.

Gavin said nothing about the calf until she had been twice round the house, wrinkling her nose at the accumulated dust, investigating everything as though she had been away for ten years and not ten days. Then he said quite casually:

"By the way, there's something I'd rather like to show you." They went out to the byre.

The calf came to Gavin as soon as it heard his voice, nuzzling at his fingers and flicking its short tail. Margaret went on her knees beside it and put her arms round its neck. It did not seem to mind, but merely went on with its busy nuzzling. She laid her cheek against the soft neck.

"It's beautiful," she murmured. "It's absolutely beautiful." She made low crooning noises and the calf liked that, for it stopped nuzzling and stood letting her gently stroke its ears.

"It's a she."

"I suppose the mother was killed," she said.

"Yes. So I brought her home. I thought you'd like——"

"This is something I've wanted ever since I was a child. This or a baby seal. It's only so awful it had to happen in this way.

But think, she might have been left to die alone." He saw tears in Margaret's eyes and put his hand on her shoulder; she pressed it with her cheek.

"She's safe here."

"What does Pusan think of her?"

"He's all right, he's only really interested in sheep. Aren't you, you ridiculous animal?" The small brown-and-white collie sitting watchful by the door grinned and wagged the tip of his bushy tail. Margaret sat back on her heels.

"We'll call her Chiquita," she announced suddenly.

"Chiquita?"

"Don't you like it?"

"Yes. Chiquita," he repeated slowly. "Yes, I do."

And so the little animal became Chiquita.

"We ought to get her a collar with a bell, like a Swiss cow, then she won't get lost. Because we can't keep her cooped up in here all day, only at nights. Surely she can wander about during the daytime? I mean she can't fall into the sea or anything, not now you've finished that fence."

"Let's buy the bell first."

Chiquita suddenly got tired and lay down in the straw, her neck outstretched like that of a dog in front of a fire.

They left her sleeping.

* * * * *

In the evening Gavin decided to go up on the Little Sister and have a look at his sheep.

"Coming, love?"

Margaret had too much to do in the kitchen. "Whatever you say, I'm sure you haven't been eating properly while I was away. You're much too thin, darling." She watched him as he routled about for his pipe and field-glasses. She loved his face with the deep-set eyes, of so dark a blue that sometimes they were close to black, and his sunburnt skin. It was the face, she often thought, of a hawk with a straight nose, if you could imagine such a thing. His mouth was wide like her own, but shut a trifle too firmly; the little white lines round the eyes and from the corners of the mouth were a shade too harsh and deep for someone of his age. The whole impression he sometimes gave was of a restless, serious tautness. He was like a gipsy, she decided, with that unruly black hair and thin sunburnt face, or a Red Indian perhaps.

"Enjoy yourself," she said. "And don't be too late back. The dinner's one that could spoil." She was dressed in her normal working clothes. Black trousers and scarlet polo-necked jersey; sometimes the jersey was blue or brown or yellow, for she liked bright colours. "Take care of yourself."

He smiled.

Late afternoon turning to evening: that was the time he liked best of all; the hour when the sun was no more than two fingers above the islands and throwing a subdued light across the golden tinfoil sea, full on the seaward slopes of the mountains.

Gavin sat with his back to a rock on the rounded summit of the Little Sister, looking down the dark ravine they called the Chasm. It was very still. He never ceased to marvel at so much silence over so vast an area. A wheatear perched on a grassy knoll, bobbing and bowing. It was good to have Margaret back, he thought, life was complete again. Then he began to think about the poachers. His eye travelled across the great wastes of mountains, dotted with shining lochans, split by the corries and glens where a thousand men could hide for weeks and never be discovered. It was all on the poachers' side. They knew when they were coming and they knew where they were going. But was it so one-sided? He broke off a twig of heather and began to chew.

For instance, what about roads? They had to use the roads. It was like in war; the wheels had to run on the roads available. How many roads were there from inland? Two. And to reach the heart of the Forest any vehicle coming along those two roads had to pass either over or beside Hump Bridge. Right then, the bridge was the place to watch. So far so good. But how to know when they were coming? He spat out the shredded twig and plucked another. How and where would they strike again? Where did they come from? Fort Henry? Inverness? Ullapool? Or were they men from much farther afield? After a while he gave it up and began to look for his sheep.

The cold eyes of the glasses inched across the face of the Big Sister, picking up the white-maggoty specks of his sheep. Across on Beinn Bhreac he found another twenty, low down in the shadows on a green square of grass, and a further half-dozen near the ruined cottage by the shore, right on the edge of the Quaking Sands. It worried him, to see them there, for even without rain the place was hideously dangerous. Countless animals had been lost there, and men too, they said.

Nothing on Sgurr Bheag, but that was a mountain for chamois, falling sheer for three hundred feet to the Wailing Loch. Nothing in the Chasm, nothing but bleached stones and small stunted trees sprouting from the slits in those cataracts of dark grey rock. Nothing round the Wailing Loch, but there never was. Except for an occasional diver or gull Gavin had never seen an animal near the place. The sheep shunned the loch as though they too found it evil; no deer ever came to play on the tiny grey beach, nor to roll happily in the warm shallows. Sometimes a solitary raven sat hunched in the branches of the half-dead alder on the island. As always, the waters of the loch were black and the place lay like an inky serpent in the deep volcanic basin, surrounded by silent grey hills, small grey *kopjes*. A few miserable birch trees huddled at the burn mouth, bending, as though in prayer, away from the prevailing winds which came tearing up the Chasm from the sea. A single dwarf rowan in full berry grew by the shore, blood-red and brilliant.

In the winter gales the west wind swooped into the deep

basin whipping the black water into a welter of peaty whiteness and filling the air with a strange and eerie wailing. Gavin had heard the sound one evening in an early misty dusk, and he had run till he reached Glenaila, and that was close on two miles. He had run with the hair rising on his head and the panic cold inside him. And he never knew why.

The only deer he had ever seen by the loch was a starving hind which had come down from the freezing tops. That had been last winter when the blizzards had raged one after another all through February and March, and the deer had even come to eat his nasturtiums, so starving had they been.

Gavin counted all the sheep he could see: a hundred and thirty-five, no, six, counting his pet, the black one with white face and leggings. No one knew where the thing had appeared from. Mike Downie had the idea it could have come from the Lake District.

"Westmorland sheep, old boy. Seen masses of the blighters in the Lake District." Gavin had pointed out it could hardly have walked all the way, but Mike had insisted.

"Surprising the things an animal can do. Never think it of 'em sometimes." Nice fellow, Mike. Large and noisy and tough, but very kind.

Deer were scattered along the top of Sgurr nan Claidheamh, not easy to spot on the darkening slope. Soon they would be moving down to the flats round Loch nan Eala, the place where the wild swans gathered later in the winter, to fill the quiet frosty nights with their strange music, like the baying of distant hounds. A happy spot much loved by animals and birds, where he had often watched the deer playing in the water or on the brilliant white sands.

He watched the deer for a few minutes, then turned to the sea, looking down at his home. Blue smoke rose straight from the kitchen chimney into the still evening and through the glass he could make out the hens scratching round the back door. Margaret came out and went across to the coalshed with a bucket. On her way back she stopped and stared up at the hills. She looked close enough to touch; he waved, but she did not see him and vanished inside. Six of his cows were lying on the little grassy knolls of the beach park, russet-red against the yellowish grass. Though he searched the ground all along the shores of the little bay he could not see the other six. As well as his three hundred sheep and Margaret's gang of hens he had these twelve outwintered cows, cross Highland, tough and hardy as their surroundings. He hoped for twelve calves from them. But then he hoped for a lot of things; he hoped for a good crop of lambs; he hoped for luck and to make enough money to pay for an up-to-date sheep-fank to replace the rough-and-ready erection he and Mike had put together; for a Land Rover, for a new hay barn, new strong fencing. He fell to thinking of all he would like to do.

The ground of Glenaila would carry up to eight hundred sheep and some forty to fifty cattle, but for that sort of scale he would have to employ a man, possibly two. Margaret was wonderful, of course, helping him, encouraging when things seemed more than usually out of control. She really loved the life, but was it fair to tie her like this? They must be able to go away together sometimes for a holiday. Then there was this question of a baby. Gavin plucked another piece of coarse grass and began to chew. When the baby arrived Margaret would never be able to go away. He frowned. That bit of marshy ground between the spur of Coraval and the sea, he'd like to drain it and bring it under the plough. There were a hundred and one things he would like to do. In his mind's eye he saw it all so clearly. And all the things he'd one day like to buy for Margaret.

Sitting here dreaming won't get things done, he thought ruefully. That was what the West Wind did to a man after a while; the soft summer wind whispering from the sea. Oh, yes, an insidious builder of dreams, that gentle little wind. Thinking of the wind, he gazed at the sea. The great rollers were forming far out in the bay beyond Glenaila, sweeping in with the whole weight of the Atlantic at their backs. Some broke a good distance from the land and came in for a long way trailing smoky white streamers; some broke just before they hit the shore and a few, timing it to perfection, crashed in thunder on the gleaming rocks, forming rainbows for an instant in the spray.

He never tired of the sea, nor of listening to its music.

The sun had sunk well below the islands, turning them to blackened cinders on the water, and there was the chill of autumn on the sea breeze. Whistling to his dog he set off homewards, going fast, jumping from rock to rock, tussock to tussock, knowing well the shortest way down.

That night as they lay in bed hearing the murmur of the lazy sea, Margaret said sleepily from her mouth in the hollow of his shoulder:

"Surely there's nothing to stop the poachers coming to Bealtuinn by boat, darling!"

His answer was equally sleepy: "There's nothing to stop them arriving by helicopter."

"Yes, they could, I suppose."

"They could land here on our beach."

"Yes." She moved against him. He kissed her ear.

Oyster-catchers flew along the tideline, calling shrilly. The deer fed secure in the darkness, and, in her straw, Chiquita slept soundly.

* * * * *

Inspector Marr took the Bealtuinn road in error and finished up at the Lodge. He wandered round the empty house, peering hopefully through the dusty windows, seeing nothing but dust-sheeted furniture. As he went back to the car, a grizzled bearded giant came out of the trees. He advanced slowly and with a certain menace in his long strides.

"Would it be me you were wanting?" He growled the question.

"Well," said Marr, "I'm looking for Glenaila Farm."

The giant jerked a thumb over his shoulder. "Glenaila's back that way." His back was hurting and he was short-tempered.

"Excuse me, but is your name Grant?"

"Aye, it is." The blue eyes looked down at Marr suspiciously.

"You're the head stalker here?"

"I am." Words were not things to be flung about with abandon.

Marr kept at it. "I see you're going to the hill." He nodded at the rifle slung on the other's massive shoulder.

"Aye."

"Bad business, this poaching."

The stalker got out a little black pipe and began to fill it with what looked like scraps of oily sacking.

"I expect you'll have had a few arguments with poachers yourself." Marr smiled in a friendly way.

Grant struck a match.

"What I can't make out," went on the Inspector hopefully, "is how the devil these chaps get away with it. No one ever seems to see them, or hear them. No one ever seems to know anything. Very odd."

Grant squinted through the billowing smoke as he drew hard on the pipe. "You know what I'm thinking is the reason," he said very deliberately.

"No, what?" The Inspector looked interested.

"It's the police." The stalker removed the pipe, spat, and replaced it.

"Oh, really. In what way?"

"They're just not wanting to get off their fat backsides and go after these bloody poachers at all. Or else they are sitting over their whisky that long they cannot——" He broke off and had another go at his pipe.

"I see," said Marr meekly.

"Now if I can be putting you on the road for Glenaila, I must be getting to the hill. There are beasts left wounded." Grant spat again. Then he watched till the car was out of sight.

"What sort of a man would that be?" he asked himself cautiously, pulling thoughtfully at his little black pipe. "Och well." He had more important things to be doing than worrying himself about silly wee men asking silly wee questions. John Grant strode away through the trees, along the path leading to the Forest.

Inspector Marr drove slowly up the Glenaila road, marvelling at the scenery. He was a man who dearly loved the country and escaped from his office at the slightest opportunity to drive or to walk or to lie on his back in the heather with his arms under his head thinking how he would rather have been anything but a policeman.

Patrick Marr was a man who by nature infinitely preferred solitude. Unmarried and without much inclination to find himself a wife, he had little family life. His father had died on the Somme, leaving a widowed mother who only survived her husband by five years. He was brought up by various well-meaning relations who left him a great deal to his own devices.

Rounding the last corner before the farm he overtook a man dressed in faded corduroy trousers and khaki shirt open at the neck and wearing heavy black shoes. A collie ran at the wheels barking furiously. The Inspector stuck his head out.

"Mr Blair?"

"That's me."

For some reason Marr took an instant liking to what he saw. "Ah, good. My name's Marr—Inspector Marr." He smiled. Not much like a policeman, Gavin thought, but probably they often weren't.

"Hop in, I'll give you a lift to your front door."

Gavin got in. "Go on, Pusan, home," he called. The dog stretched out at his fullest speed.

"God's sakes," exclaimed Marr admiringly, "that dog can move all right. Shave him and you could palm him off as a blooming greyhound. Nice little place you've got here. Must be a bit lonely in the winter though."

"Not if you're married."

"Ah, no."

They took a stroll round. Gavin was surprised at how much the man seemed to know about the country. They chatted about sheep and birds and the sea, and the Inspector grew animated as he spoke of the things obviously so close to his heart and his rather prominent brown eyes lit up with enthusiasm.

"I suppose you get a good few deer round you when the snow comes?"

"In the bad storms they come right down to the house and start poking about in the dustbin."

"Do they really? Wish I'd more time to come out and watch them. Of course, I've read everything I can lay my hands on, Fraser Darling, the lot. But it's not the same." He leant with his back to the sheep fence, looking up at the great rounded summit of Beinn Bhreac.

"Magnificent," he murmured. "Quite magnificent."

In his worn tweed suit and stained tweed cap he could have been a good-natured, ruddy-faced farmer. He removed the cap and hung it on the post beside him, revealing a head of thinning brown hair, going grey. Gavin pointed to the sunlight on Coraval.

"See that big green patch like a pony's head?"

The Inspector nodded, screwing up his eyes.

"Well, just above it, d'you see them?"

"No."

The specks moved on to a lighter patch.

"Ah, now I do. Good lord, yes. Like a lot of lice, aren't they?"

The deer were feeding slowly into the wind, about thirty of them.

"They're pretty hard to pick up sometimes. I've watched till my eyes hurt and couldn't see a thing, yet I knew they were there. A sudden change of light, a shadow, or they go on to a darker background and they might as well be invisible."

"Fascinating," said Marr. "Absolutely fascinating. By crackers, I envy you living here."

"I wouldn't change it. See the trees on that little cliff?"

Marr looked up at the scrubby larches clinging to the lip of the crag.

"I've counted up to forty stags feeding there. Don't know how on earth they get up there."

"Forty!" The Inspector whistled. "That's a thing I'd like to see."

"You must come out for a day and we'll go to the top of the Little Sister. That one, the one with a heap of rocks on the top. There's quite a view on a clear day."

"Thanks very much. I'd love to." Marr mopped his broad face. "There's still a lot of heat in that sun. You'd hardly think it was practically October."

"I know. But it can change in an afternoon. When the blizzards come, then it's not quite so idyllic."

"This is my first winter up here. I'm from the Borders myself. It can be pretty rough down there in a February storm, but not so——" he searched for the right words. "Well, not so savage as this area." He offered a cigarette. "No? Lucky man. I've been trying to stop for the last ten years."

He smoked in silence. A trawler crept along the horizon and Gavin could see gannets plummeting into the green sea off the Mermaids. The Inspector smoked his cigarette and envied the possession of such a—such a paradise.

"You had a bit of excitement the other night," he said quietly.

"A change from the daily chores, yes."

"So I'd imagine." Marr picked up a small stone which he tossed up and down on the palm of his hand. "This is where I combine business with pleasure," he remarked. "Would you like to tell me what happened? I've read the report, of course. Constable McPhail's. Whom God preserve, amen. But I'd rather like to hear it first hand, from the horse's mouth so to speak. If you've no objection."

"None at all."

"Splendid."

They sat on a grassy knoll at the edge of the little beach and Gavin told him the tale. The Inspector lay on his back with his eyes shut. Gavin finished. He thought Marr was asleep, but the policeman sat up.

"Not much to go on, but that's not your fault. A van. How many vans between here and Inverness, for instance?" Gavin watched his new Shetland rams, Simon and Peter, grazing contentedly in the sunshine.

"We know who takes the venison and can't do a damned thing about it. The stuff's not stolen property—not legally, that is. So we can't run in Macsquash the butcher for taking deer he knows to have been poached." He threw the stone into the sparkling sea.

"A lot of people think we're too slow to catch a cold in the head. You're probably one of them. Can't say I blame you. That stalker chap over at Bealtuinn—Grant? Yes, well, in his view we're as much good as a bunch of blasted pickled onions in a jar. Pretty well told me so this morning. I took the wrong road and ended up at his place. God help us, the fool can't even find his way about, how the devil's he hoping to catch anybody?" He laughed. Then he chucked another stone into the water.

"Plop, and it's gone, just like that. A big place, the Atlantic. This Forest's a big place too. How do you begin?"

"Presumably the only hope is to catch them with the dead beasts actually in the car or van or whatever it is."

"Exactly. And even then you can't be sure of a conviction. Only the other day a couple of the sods were found with a hind stuffed into the boot of the car, not even dead, poor brute. What happens? Not proven." The Inspector snorted angrily.

"This new Act they're talking about, surely that'll help?"

"May do. I doubt it. We'll see when the first case comes up. Of course, on paper the penalties are going to be a good deal stiffer. Up to six months inside. That's no sort of a joke, you know."

"If they're ever used," said Gavin, adding: "I wonder why the law is so much harder on salmon poaching for instance."

"Salmon don't interfere with people's livelihoods, crops and what-not. They don't chew up corn and turnips. That's one of the reasons," said Marr shrewdly. "They only bring in the lolly, they don't take it out of people's pockets." He rubbed his fingers and thumb together. "It's all this, you know. No, between you and me and that boat out there it's a pretty frustrating business running in deer poachers. Or so my colleagues tell me. But these chaps now, the ones you tangled with, they're a different story. They shot at you. And that's something we *could* get them for. Now if they'd hit you . . ." he said wistfully.

"Thanks very much. You'd like me to play guinea-pig, is that it?"

The Inspector threw back his head and laughed loudly. "Not a bad idea. Think they'll come back?"

Gavin thought for a moment. "Yes, I do. The place is stiff with deer at the moment and as soon as the hard weather sets in they'll be milling all over the low ground near the roads just asking to be shot."

"It struck me that perhaps the poachers would avoid the

roads altogether. I mean, why not leave the vehicle a goodish way off and come in on foot, shoot the deer, cut 'em up and cart the meat out on their backs?"

Gavin shook his head. "You've got to be damned tough to carry a heavy load over this ground, and in the dark too."

"Mm—yes, I suppose so. Only an idea. You'll find I'm bang full of fairly useless ideas."

Marr looked at his watch, got to his feet. "Must be on my way."

"Come in and have a drink. My wife's somewhere about in the house and she likes an occasional new face. Why not stay and have some lunch?"

"No, don't bother her, I'll look in another day when I've got more time. Thanks all the same." They walked slowly back to the car.

"Well then, it looks as if all we can do is to wait and see," said Marr. "But let me know if anything turns up, anything at all. You'd be surprised how the very smallest thing can help us. Let me know through Constable McPhail, whom God preserve. Can't have people going over his head. A very conscientious man if not a hundred per cent quicksilver. Between you and me and this steering-wheel the law is under strength in Bealtuinn at the moment. What earthly use is a bicycle? He should be mobile, not creaking about on a blooming penny-farthing thing. Well, very nice to have met you——" He pressed the starter. "Call in any day you're in Fort Henry. Oh, and by the way, don't go trying anything on your own. Nothing drastic, I mean. Someone might get hurt, and the law takes a poor view of people getting hurt—even if they deserve it. Not to mention actions for unlawful assault and all that sort of thing. Pity in some ways, but there we are. Take that case the other day when a chap caught some poachers on his place in the middle of the night. They turned a spotlight on him and he shot it out. What's the result? He gets a stiffer sentence than the poachers. Quite right he should in some ways. If everyone began taking the law into their own hands, then where'd we be? State of blasted anarchy all round."

"Sometimes I think a bit of full-blooded anarchy wouldn't do any harm."

"I can imagine how you feel about all this . . ."

"What I feel, what a great many people feel, is that the law should be altered and that this type of poaching should be recognised for what it is—filthy cruelty—and punished accordingly. These poachers are ruthless. All right then, deal with them in the same way and you'd find the whole thing would damn soon stop."

Inspector Marr regarded the other's fierce anger and thought, You feel strongly, don't you? And you're the kind of man who'll do something about it—and probably get yourself into trouble doing it.

"I sometimes think," he said, "that if all of you got together over things like this, you'd make a blooming nonsense of the law." He laughed but spoke seriously. "Don't think I'm not sympathising with your point of view. I am, strongly—as a private individual. But I'm a policeman." With a brisk nod and wave the Inspector drove away.

Gavin stood, thinking over what he had said, then turned towards the house. Margaret appeared, shaking a duster from an upper window.

"Who was that, darling?"

"A police inspector."

"Police inspector? He didn't look much like one, did he, in that baggy old suit. What did he want? I thought he'd come to sell you sheep-dip or something. He had a nice face."

"He was a nice man. He was talking about the poachers."

"Oh." She vanished inside, then popped back, this time with a broom.

"Is Chiquita all right? I saw her wandering off towards the rams, they won't hurt her, will they, darling?"

"No, of course not."

"What's the time?"

"Nearly twelve."

"Oh, goodness, time for her bottle, she'll be ravenous." Her small head vanished again. Gavin walked down to inspect the rams. Chiquita was standing on straddled legs peering at them from a distance. Margaret arrived with the bottle, calling softly to the calf. Chiquita uttered a short excited bleat and trotted unsteadily towards food. She sucked rapturously, with her eyes tight shut and her tail going like a tiny pendulum. Milk dribbled down into the pale fur of her throat.

"She's growing," said Margaret firmly. "Definitely. I wonder if her collar's too tight? No, I don't think so. By the way, darling, I saw Mike in the shop. He's coming for a drink on Friday. I told him about seven. I knew you'd probably be late if you're going out to the sheep."

"How was he?"

"Deafening as usual. No, Chiquita, that's all." The bottle drained dry, the calf wandered off to join the rams, who paid her no more attention than a brief goggle-eyed glance.

"She's very much one of the family now, isn't she? Aren't you rather glad you found her?"

"Yes, I am, very. Especially if she gives you all this pleasure." Gavin bent to kiss the top of his wife's head. They watched the little animal as she tried vainly to get the rams to play, then he took her hand and they walked to the house.

[4]

DURING the next three days the weather changed and bitter black frosts fell from the cold starlit skies. But in the daytime the sun softened the iron ground and laid a coating of silver dust upon the crackly grass. Gavin, busy with the preparation of fenced ground in the shelter of Coraval, heard the first roaring of the stags and, one night, the first wild music of the geese as they passed through the darkness to the loch.

He was working very hard: from soon after dawn until well after the sun had dropped below the darkening rim of the sea. At midday Margaret brought him sandwiches and coffee and often stayed to help with the work. Sometimes she brought Chiquita with her and the calf made no attempt to run away; she would wander a little way up the hillside, but it obviously frightened her to be far from Margaret and she would soon come scampering back to safety.

By the fourth day the task was complete; the fence was up, the troughs in place, a certain amount of shelter ready for the sheep he would drive down from the mountains when the first blizzard threatened. As reward he took his glass and climbed to the summit of Beinn Bhreac. He had wanted Margaret to go with him but she had stayed to prepare for the evening.

"Mike's bound to stay for dinner, he always makes an evening of it, and you know how he eats. Don't be too late back, will you? He's such a handful by oneself."

"Back by half-past six."

Gavin leant against the boulder at the top, the one that looked like a crouching man from below. The sunlight struck slanting across the flat, pale sea; half a dozen seals sunned themselves on the Devil's Knucklebones and a great assembly of gulls was gathered on the grass by the ruined cottage. He could just see a narrow strip of the Wailing Loch, black between the Sisters. There was that flat, blue haze which often hangs like smoke across the mountains and makes observation so difficult. But his glass picked up a big stag—a black stag he'd seen before—low down on Creag Dhu, running among his hinds.

Resting the glass on his raised knees he settled down to watch. He saw the beast stretch out his neck and roar three times, and seconds later the anguished sound reached across the distance. It was the bellowing roar of a bullock, the coughing snarl of a lion, finishing in a succession of angry rasping grunts.

Since daybreak the black stag had been trying to shepherd his scattered harem towards the Cave of the Laughing Men. Sixty passive females waiting for their lord and master to run among them and pick them one by one as mates; they stooped their heads for quick snatches at the grass, raising them to watch for other stags. They did not mind with which stag they mated. The bravest, the boldest, the strongest—he it was who got the fair. So he roared from his grossly swollen throat, this big stag in the pride of his strength, and the breath sprayed as fine mist from his outstretched muzzle.

He was thin, almost emaciated, and blackened by wallowing in the peat-hags; the hair of his chest was matted and clotted with mud, the cage of his ribs showed clearly and his belly was fallen in, arching up to his fiery, insatiable loins. A beast of seven autumns and of long experience. For a week now, since the coming of the frost, he had satisfied a great number of hinds, having no time for food or rest, and he was worn by the continual running with the females. He had no leisure for anything but the frantic efforts to guard his hinds from the other stags and to mate with them time after time in a vain attempt to tame the frenzy of his lust.

So he ran this way and that, roaring, scything at the moss

with his antlers so that the points were white as polished ivory; he rolled in the glutinous peat-holes to cool himself. Often he had to run out at some impudent youngster and then, as soon as that one had turned tail, back to the other flank of the clustered hinds to repel another raid. Gavin watched the stag as he skilfully headed a rival, moving along the hillside, parallel and always above; then the sudden savage charge downhill and the other animal blundering away from the long points aimed at his side.

When the little drama was played out and the deer had vanished behind a knoll, Gavin turned to business, to searching for his sheep. A large number were scattered beyond the road to the east of Coraval, where they should be. But a few were dotted high on the Big Sister, lulled by the windless sunshine. If a storm came, those would be the ones he'd lose. Tomorrow he'd get them down. But they would wander, that was the worst of good weather at the back-end of autumn: it scattered the sheep all over the place. There were more on the Little Sister and a long file moving slowly up the Black Burn. He counted a hundred and twenty-nine in all.

Gavin swung the glass across the sunset sea but saw no boats. Surf creamed round the Knucklebones, pink in the lowering sun which winked from the lighthouse glass. It was suddenly very cold. He blew on his fingers and stamped his feet.

"Time to go, Pusan," he said aloud. The collie smiled as only an intelligent dog can, with his head on one side, ears cocked and the breath steaming round his gleaming, grinning teeth. He ran with his master down the hill, jumping and frisking. They did not head for home but towards the mouth of the Black Burn where Gavin had also spotted sheep near the Quaking Sands. If they were quick they could drive them to safety before dark and go back by the shore path.

But half-way down the dog stopped and stood motionless staring ahead, with the hair rising on his shoulders. Looking along the line of the pointing head, Gavin made out the ears of a hind visible above the grass. She was facing away, downhill. Signalling the dog to heel, he went forward very slowly, stepping as though in a minefield and never taking his eyes off the ears which began to twitch and move. Her head was turning, first left, then right, but not behind, and they got to within a few yards before she staggered to her feet. One front leg dangled useless and smashed at the knee. She stood for a moment trying to make out the danger so close to her, then she uttered a short bark and hobbled away on her three legs.

There was blood where she had been lying and hairs smeared across a rock. The hind did not go far and for the second time he got close; so close that he thought she must be blinded, but her face was unscarred. The short hobbling rushes seemed to tire the poor creature, for each time her head drooped and Gavin thought she was going to fall. He wondered if Pusan could pull her down. The dog crouched, belly to ground, as he did when herding sheep, never taking his yellow eyes off her. But Gavin had no knife, no means of ending her suffering. Try and drive her into the Chasm, that was the answer, then he would know where to find her in the morning. Slowly they drove her before them, and each time she stopped Gavin thought she was done, but each time the wounded beast used a little more of her dwindling strength to totter away into the dusk.

Soon it was too dark to see the hind. She would lie down; perhaps she would die. In the morning he would come and find her. Gavin took the track through the Chasm, heading for the Wailing Loch. The tops of the ravine were flooded with moonlight, but the path was in deeper darkness. Very slowly the harsh white light crept down one side, leaving the other black and menacing. Somewhere, a long way off, a stag roared and another one answered, much nearer. The sides of the Chasm towered above him, pressing in as mountains do at night, roofed by a narrow strip of starlit sky.

The clatter on the rocks was sharp, low down in the shadows. He froze, feeling very naked in the moonlight. Pusan growled.

"Sst!" Gavin held him tightly. They listened, and the dog heard more in the silence for he quivered and strained to escape. A sudden blink of light flashed on the dark slope, boots slithered on loose scree, then complete silence. Nothing moved. In all that waste of white light and black shadow, nothing moved. The sound had come from the steep gully, a chimney of scree and boulders, leading to the top. He heard a whisper, plain as a shout in the silence.

"Let's get out of 'ere!" The boots clattered again; stones rattled down. With a fierce leap Pusan was away, streaking for the gully. Gavin ran after him, tripped and fell, scrambled to his feet hearing the ugly sounds of his dog attacking.

"Christ, get 'im 'orf!" The man yelled with pain and anger; Pusan was snarling viciously.

The blast of the shot was deafening, magnified by the darkness and the steep cliffs. He ducked at the whine of the ricochet but ran on.

"You bloody fool!" he shouted.

Gavin caught a glimpse of two figures climbing above him and the body of his dog, lying very still. The men paused on the skyline, then vanished. He knew it was no good trying to go after them.

The dog was breathing very faintly and there was blood sticky all over his head. Gavin spoke as he would have done to a wounded man, encouraging and soothing. Pusan tried to raise his head; his tail thumped feebly. Gavin carried him home and the journey took over an hour, for the dog was heavy and the going not easy. In fact, if Mike Downie had not met him below the Big Sister Gavin would not have been back much before eight.

"Poor old Margaret's having kittens. Thought I'd better

come out and have a *shufti*. What the hell's been going on?" They put the dog gently on the back seat.

"Poachers. In the Chasm. Pusan went for one of them and got shot at."

"Trigger-happy bastards." Mike turned the car in a roaring spray of stones. "What happened to 'em?"

"I'm afraid they got away. We'd better report it, I suppose."

"Won't do much good, old boy. They'll be half across Scotland by now. No, you and I have got to cram our thinking caps on and get down to a bit of planning or these characters'll start thinking they own the ruddy place. What d'you think they were up to?"

"God knows! I didn't hear any shots."

"Reconnaissance?"

"Could have been. I'll have a thorough look round tomorrow."

Margaret was standing by the gate.

"I was beginning to wonder if we'd be seeing each other again." She kissed him and held him tight for a moment.

"Don't you worry about him, Margaret," roared Mike. "Nothing ever happens to the bad pennies." He lifted Pusan out of the car.

"Gavin, what's happened? Oh, he's hurt." She ran forward.

"Not to worry," Mike assured her. "He's all right. Stunned, that's all. Lucky it wasn't your good husband here."

They took the dog indoors and laid him on a bath towel before the fire. Margaret cut away the clotted hair and bathed the wound.

"An inch lower and he'd have had it." Mike drank his whisky and offered advice. He was right: an inch lower and the bullet would have torn through the brain. In the warmth, revived by the milk and brandy and the soft flow of sympathy from Margaret, the dog soon shook off the effects of the blow and staggered unsteadily to his feet, wagging his tail and trying hard to grin.

"Well done," encouraged Mike. "That dog's got guts all right. And he's achieved more than anyone else has." He held up the scrap of bloodstained cloth removed from Pusan's teeth.

"There's one of them won't be feeling too comfortable anyway."

The collie's eyes brightened with pleasure at the tone. He lay down again with his head on his paws. Chiquita advanced very cautiously from her laundry basket in the corner and touched the dog's face gently with her wet nose.

"Good grief, look at that! Pally as you like." The little bell tinkled as the calf raised her head. Her spotted coat was glossy in the lamplight that shone in her great eyes. She nuzzled the dog's neck and skipped back. She stood with her legs wide, raising and lowering her head and snuffling.

"No, Chiquita, he doesn't want to play, not now." Margaret put her back in the basket where she lay peering over the top, looking puzzled. Gavin came back from the telephone.

"Well, what did the law have to say?"

"Much as usual. That he will be reporting the matter to Fort Henry and coming out to see me—in the morning, Mr Blair, to be getting a statement from you, etcetera etcetera. The usual stuff."

"What's the use of that?" said Margaret hotly.

"Have a heart, darling. There's not much else he could do."

She sat staring angrily into the fire. "I know. But it's all so—I don't know, nothing ever seems to get done, oh, I can't explain."

"Tin hats in wear," boomed Mike suddenly. "Quite like old days, eh? Bullets zipping about the place. Well, by God, if it's trouble they want, then they can damn well have it. Hell, I've knocked off better men than these and been paid to do it. I'd put a slug into one of those jokers, soon as look at 'em. Poor old Pusan." He took another long pull at his glass. He was a large and hefty man, Michael Alexander Downie, with a large voice, receding reddish hair and a short scrubby moustache. Buried somewhere underneath his hearty noisy exterior was a certain shrewd intelligence and the ruthless streak of the hard-bitten professional fighting man. His eyes were small and grey and lively; there was a very firm set to his mouth and jaw. The ragged line of a scar ran down the side of his strong sunburnt neck. He had been a soldier for fifteen years of his life, of the private-army type, and he now lived alone at Famista, farming sheep and hill cattle and apparently quite content with his solitary existence.

His check waistcoat was undone and his broad face scarlet from firelight and whisky; his long legs were stuck out with the boat-like shoes almost in the embers.

"What's to be done then?" he asked. Margaret looked up from patting Pusan. "You've told old Donald and you've had his answer. Now what? Dead end. As far as I can see, it'll go on being a dead end till we do something about it ourselves."

"I agree. I mean—as you said yourself, Gavin—what *can* Donald do? Poor old thing, pedalling about on that ridiculous rattletrap bicycle, talking about section this, that and the other."

"He does his best," said Gavin.

"Not enough, old boy. Not for this sort of lark. Speed's what's needed. Speed and more speed. Action and punch and what have you. Oh, I say, jolly good, I've gone and sloshed me drink all over the place."

Gavin remembered the Inspector's words. "Vigilantes, that's what we'll be. You and me and John. Kenny. Might even get Doc in on it, and the Minister, he's quite a truculent type."

"Yes," said Margaret. "If there's action to be taken, then it looks as if we'll have to be the ones to take it."

"Bravo, Maggie, that's the spirit." At times Mike had the distressing habit of calling her Maggie.

"What about you, darling, you're very quiet all of a sudden?"

Gavin took his time in answering. He was a person who liked to get things well worked out before putting forward suggestions; he liked to cut down argument to the minimum.

"I was thinking. To begin with we're obviously at a disadvantage not knowing (*a*) where they come from and (*b*) when they are coming. But one thing I think we can be certain of and that is, they'll try again."

"Agreed," said Mike. Margaret nodded.

"Right, then. How will they come? By road, by sea or on foot? My guess is road."

"They'd never make it on foot. Not carting a ruddy great load of meat."

"Exactly. That's what I told the Inspector. And unless they've got hold of a skipper who knows this coast like the back of his hand they're not likely to try and land, except when there's not a breath of wind."

"And then surely only in about three places," put in Margaret.

Gavin nodded agreement. "Glenaila. Bealtuinn. Seal Bay and possibly Truina when the tide's right and the swell down to nothing." He counted on his fingers.

"Even if they landed, they'd never get the dead animals out to the boat. I think you're right, old boy, the roads are the main things to watch."

"Hump Bridge," said Gavin. "That's the key point. Hang on, I'll get a map."

"After we've had something to eat."

"Good girl, Maggie, that's the stuff."

When the meal was finished they cleared everything off the table and spread out the map. By the end of half an hour they had reached certain conclusions. The main one was this: the only vantage point from where they could overlook the sea, the bridge and both the roads was the summit of the Little Sister.

"What we'll have to do," said Gavin, "is to organise some

system of watching. We've got glasses and telescopes and we know the country pretty well."

"Standing patrols, eh?"

"That sort of thing, yes."

Margaret brought coffee. They discussed the idea at some length. Mike got noisier and noisier, till finally a terrified Chiquita left her basket and came to Margaret's side for comfort.

"You're frightening her out of her wits."

"I say, I'm very sorry." Mike raised his glass to the startled calf and said solemnly: "Your amazing good health, Chiquita." The calf gazed at him with her soft, frightened eyes. They talked on.

"What we really need, of course, are two or three different observation points and some form of intercommunication so that whoever sees anything can call the others."

"Walkie-talkies," said Mike. "Nothing like the good old walkie-talkie."

"What on earth is that? It sounds like something to do with Charlie Chaplin." Margaret laughed.

"Wirelesses. Small portable wirelesses carried on people's backs."

"What fun!"

"With a couple of those things we'd soon fix these chaps. Mobile force standing by. Pincer movements, covering fire, the lot." Mike was waxing enthusiastic. "We've got plenty of vehicles. Maggie can keep us going with an inexhaustible supply of black coffee and cheese sandwiches." He broke off suddenly and sat frowning.

"The snag is how to spare the time. Robbie's off with 'flu or measles or something and I've got to get that ruddy sheep-fank finished before the weather breaks, poachers or no poachers."

"No sign of that," Gavin said. "The glass is steady as a rock. We're safe for another day or so."

"Hadn't you better discuss all this with John?" suggested Margaret.

"Good grief, yes. He knows every stone on the place. Besides, he's itching to have a crack at them himself."

"What I want to know," said Margaret from where she sat with Pusan's head in her lap, "is where they get rid of the deer. I mean, who buys them?"

"Butchers, dealers, potted-meat factories. A good number of carcases go to Germany, poached and legitimate, it doesn't matter, there's always a market for dead deer."

"Well then, can't *they* be arrested or prosecuted, these butchers and potted-meat factories and——"

Mike let out a bellow of laughter. "I'd give a lot to see you arresting a potted-meat factory." He slapped his leg.

"I'm afraid it's not a crime to deal in poached venison," said Gavin.

"Then all I can say is it's time it was made one."

"Difficult to prove, darling," he said gently. He could see she was getting angry; a flush was spreading across her neck and that was always a bad sign.

"The thing is," she burst out, "that no one cares. No one *really* cares. Just think of the fuss and hysteria there'd be if the precious grouse were poached like this, by gangs feeding them on poisoned berries or something and selling them in hundreds all over the place. We'd never hear the end of it. All the shiny country magazines would be bulging with letters and articles. New laws would be rushed in helter-skelter and the poachers would be sent to prison for years and years."

"Whoa-ho, Maggie! What about this new Act they're bringing in?"

"I don't know anything about that, but I do know it's all because the deer eat a few mangy turnips or oats and so nobody cares a penny piece what happens to them, they can be murdered and wounded all over the place and people say oh dear, how terrible, and forget it."

"That's not quite fair, Margaret," said Gavin quietly. "They do a lot of damage one way and another. What about the crofter who sees his crops being ruined? He's got no particular reason for being fond of the deer."

"That's no excuse for just sitting back and allowing the poachers to do what they like."

"I know it's no excuse, darling. But you can see the crofters and farmers aren't likely to care much if some of the deer are killed off. They aren't going to mind who does it either."

"Nor how," she added bitterly.

"No, if people's pockets are touched, then nobody's going to make much fuss at the deer being killed. You're right, darling, it doesn't matter who does the killing, that's what it boils down to."

"She's got something there, old boy." Mike was staring at her small angry face with stolid admiration. "Look at the forestry blokes. Want to shoot everything that moves, just to guard their ruddy trees."

"And the seals," she added. "They'll wipe them out too if they get half a chance, so there can be a few more salmon for people to go and hook."

"I know. I know. I agree entirely with both of you. I was merely——"

But his wife did not let him finish. "We go all sentimental over dogs and cats and horses, man's best friends and so on. We drool over hamsters and koala bears and poodle puppies, aren't they too cuddly for words and aren't we so gentle and kindhearted to them. But the deer aren't anyone's friends—well, they are if you give them the chance, look at Chiquita." At her name the calf appeared over the rim of the basket, the straw crackling as she moved. "To most people they're just romantic pictures all draped in heather and mist, or stuffed heads in perfectly hideous houses."

"You say nobody cares. You're wrong, y'know, Maggie. The stalkers care."

"The stalkers! How many stalkers are there in Scotland? They can't do anything."

"They could if they all got together."

"If!"

Gavin leant forward and touched her shoulder. "Don't take it so hard, darling."

She put her hand on his. "I know. I'm sorry. It's just that it makes me so sick to see these brutes paying silly little fines and being told by some spineless little sheriff, 'You can have a chance this time and the next time, *and* the time after that, oh what horrid, naughty boys you've been.' Now I've talked enough."

"By jove!" That was all Mike could say. The grandfather clock at the bottom of the stairs whirred and rattled and finally struck midnight.

"Good grief, I say, listen to that. Me for Schloss Downie and a spot of Bedfordshire." He lumbered to his feet.

"Busy day tomorrow. Up at four. A gathering of the Downie sheep, all half a dozen of them. Well, thanks for the meal, Maggie. Can't get me fancy waistcoat done up, never can after your cooking." He patted Pusan. "Wound stripe for old collie." He blew a noisy kiss to Chiquita. As he was shrugging into his ancient British warm he said: "Better fix a day to see John and get things tied up. Synchronise watches, gentlemen. We'll make out a roster. Downie four till six, Blair six till twelve, ha-ha."

They stood by the jeep as he heaved himself in. The sky was ablaze with the Northern Lights, flickering, fading, filling the heavens with brilliant pulsating light. At one moment a wide fan of green, red and golden yellow, then changing as they watched to searchlight beams probing the outer darkness; eerie shimmering fingers stabbing at the southern sky.

"Up the Merry Dancers," yelled Mike. "Just look at 'em, riding the Lights up there. By jove, what a sight! But I don't like it, old boy. Not when they're in the south. Dirty weather brewing, mark old Downie's word." Suddenly he bellowed at the very pitch of his powerful lungs. "The M-e-e-rry Da-a-ncers!"

The wild sound echoed away among the shadowy hills. Pusan howled feebly from inside the house. On the hidden slopes of Coraval stags were roaring.

"Lucky devils, all the wives in the world and no ruddy income tax. Well, keep me posted, old boy. You're C-in-C this operation. Soon as possible."

"Not tomorrow," put in Margaret firmly. "We're going to Seal Bay for our Saturday picnic. Probably the last one before the cold weather."

"Monday then?"

"If I can get hold of John, yes. I'll let you know on Sunday evening. All right?"

"Fine. Well, night-night all. Many thanks for——" The jeep shot away through the gate.

"Lights!" They shouted in unison. An arm waved. The headlights split the night. They stood for a moment watching the Merry Dancers weaving their fantastic patterns across the sky.

"Poor Mike, he must be awfully lonely at times."

"Yes, I think he must." His arm went round her waist. "A man without a woman is only half a man—provided she's the right one, that is."

He saw the quick gleam of her smile. She brushed his cheek with her lips. After a moment's silence she said: "Darling, I'm sorry, I'm afraid I rather lost control of myself."

"You've nothing to be sorry about."

"But I can't help it, not when I think about the animals."

"I know, Margaret, and I love you for it."

The sea was smooth as polished glass but the eternal swell of the Atlantic surged and hissed without pause over the stones. They listened, her head on his shoulder. Then they turned and went inside.

* * * * *

Gavin found the hind near where he had last seen her. It was not difficult to get close for she was too weak to stand. He shot her cleanly through the neck and she fell on her side, stone dead. After she was gralloched he wiped his hands and arms with moss and then sat for a while in the early morning sunlight. The Wailing Loch was black and smooth as ink; the sun struck through the dawn mists hanging in the hollows and turned the summit of Beinn Bhreac to the colour of a lion's skin. He could just make out the distant glint of the sea beyond the Truina Sands. Stags were roaring all over the Forest; a raven croaked as it swooped to investigate the killing, and its harsh cry echoed between the great walls of the Chasm. Grouse whirred and clucked like cars starting up and a curlew flew above him complaining sadly.

He lay back among the frosted cobwebs of dew, savouring the moment, staring up through half-shut eyes at the scattered little clouds, still faintly stained from the flaring sunrise. The curlew returned, flying slowly and uttering its plaintive, haunting call, as though searching for something. A few autumn flies buzzed round the dead hind; a very small mouse popped its head out from a tuft of heather, then vanished with a tiny rustle. Gavin felt like singing or shouting his joy at the vast peace and beauty of the morning. But instead he got to his feet, covered the hind with stones and heather and climbed slowly up the gully to where Pusan had been shot. He searched in the scree but found nothing. At some time in the night there must have been a light shower of rain or perhaps it was the dew, anyway he could see no spots of blood, nor even the empty case. He climbed to the top and stood looking out across the Forest. Long curtains of white mist hung in the valleys and clung here and there to the sides of the mountains. The sea was the colour of jade. He would have liked to sit down and chew a piece of heather and just gaze over that lonely mountainous land for hours on end.

But today was the day for their picnic. And what a day it promised to be. After one last look round he made his way back to Glenaila.

[5]

THEY toiled up the last few feet and at the top of the hillock Margaret flung herself down in the heather, gasping and laughing.

"Goodness, the heat!"

It was still unseasonably hot and the hazy sky was clear of cloud except low down on the sea where a dark bar lay along the horizon. She spread out the rug. For a little while they lay getting their breath back. Then Gavin leant over on one elbow and kissed his wife in the hollow of her throat.

"Thank you, darling," she said. Her arms went round his neck and pulled his face close to hers.

"I'm really rather fond of you, Margaret," he whispered.

"You are?"

In answer he kissed her on the lips. Presently he sat up and gazed about him, stretching in the warm sunshine. Below where they sat was the ruined cottage surrounded by the grey remains of other broken walls and rich green grass patched with sphagnum moss. A golden line of seaweed swayed and shimmered in the surge of the ebbing tide. Beyond the shallow curve of white sand stretched the Bay of Splashing Seals, green as a bottle held to the light. Less than fifty yards away the Quaking Sands lay shining among tufts of rushes, peaceful and silent and deadly as a sheathed blade. Herring gulls chuckled coldly on the rocks and on the little grassy knolls along the shore.

Insects murmured in the midday heat and Pusan lay panting with droplets of water falling from his tongue and his eyes half closed, the strip of plaster stuck to his head like a little rakish cap. Gavin took his glass and spied up the Glen of the Skull. Deer were dotted on Beinn Gobhair, visible to the naked eye if you knew where to look, and when they moved the sun turned them to spots of dark gold. A single stag roared at the entrance to the Chasm and a long file of sheep was making its way up the burn path. He watched a party of eider duck rising and falling on the lazy swell. A man came out of the lighthouse door on to the top of the steps; he hung a pair of trousers on the washing line, stared at a trawler making along the coast and went back inside. Gavin snapped shut the glass.

"There's something piling up out there," he said.

"Never mind, darling. It's much too fine to think of storms." She sat up and peeled off her blue cardigan. Rolling it into a pillow she lay back, sweeping her hand through the heather tops so that her white shirt and faded blue jeans were dusted with brown debris. Her ankles were bare and her feet hidden in rope-soled canvas shoes.

"You're dressed for the Mediterranean."

"This is much more beautiful," she answered. In her wide gesture she included the sea, the great glen cutting through the mountains behind them, the sky and the buzzard floating on broad wings; the deer, the sheep, the drowsy hum of insects and the clean smell of the heather. Rabbits were playing by the old sheep-fank, chasing each other and thinking in their simple way it was a day in spring. Four ravens circled and swooped like black darts, crying harshly.

"Look darling, there, by the boat." Seal heads were bobbing close to the 'Sea Parrot' and they could hear the snuffles and snorts of the inquisitive animals. "I suppose the dinghy's all right?" The little boat tugged at its long mooring line, unable to escape on the falling tide.

"Fine," he said, without looking.

"I'd give a lot to be able to paint that sea," Margaret said.

"Mm," he said sleepily. "This bay's a pretty good place, isn't it?" That was all he said, but she understood.

They unpacked the basket and ate their picnic lunch in contented silence. Afterwards they lazed in the sun; Gavin slept and when he woke he told his wife the story of the ruins by the shore.

Many years ago, or so the story went, the inhabitants of the little settlement had been trapped and put to the sword by men who came over the mountains. It was said that on stormy nights the sounds of the great killing were to be heard above the roar of the wind and sea; they said that to this day many of the rocks were still stained with the blood that no rain could wash away, and that the Quaking Sands concealed many of the dead.

Then at the turn of the century two brothers, strangers to the district and careless of legend, came home from the sea. They brought money with them; they built a house and bought sheep and cattle. Their ambition was to turn the Glen of the Skull into a thriving place where a living could be made. The brothers owned a big boat in which they were to carry their produce to the markets of the south. All prospered with them until one day the heavy after-swell of a storm capsized their boat, drowning them and all their beasts, out there at the entrance to the Bay of the Splashing Seals.

Since that day the cottage had remained empty, slowly falling apart, for it was noticed how swiftly disaster struck at those who had gone secretly to loot.

"It's not a very cosy spot, even on a day like this." Margaret shivered. "Think of it in winter, at night."

"The feel of the place reaches you even quite a way off-shore. Not exactly evil and not exactly haunted."

"Eerie," she said.

"Yes, eerie. And restless."

A feeling often to be found in the Highlands and one unknown anywhere else in the world.

"Funnily enough the deer don't mind coming here, yet you never get them at the Wailing Loch. I've counted over fifty milling about on the grass in the early morning."

"D'you remember the calf we watched? The one that came right down into the water to get a better look at us? And the expression on his face when the wind changed and he smelt us?" They talked of the early-morning expeditions in their boat and of the things they had seen and enjoyed together.

"You love this place, don't you?" she asked.

"As much as you do, yes," he said.

"You'd do anything to stop it being spoilt." It was not a question.

"I would."

She sat up and leant forward hugging her knees. "Why have these men come here, darling? Why must everything always be killing and cruelty? It was all so perfect before, and now——" Her eyes were troubled as she gazed across the sea. He put his hand on her arm.

"We'll stop them," he said. "I don't quite know how, but we will. I promise you."

"Then the deer will be safe and the place beautiful again, without fear and—and—horror."

"Yes, love."

Gavin felt the sea-wind stronger on his face.

"The sea's beginning to move. We'll have to start back."

"Not yet, darling. Don't let's go. Not just yet."

But he pulled her to her feet. They packed the basket and went down to the beach. The dark line of cloud had become a black wall rising from the horizon; the wind no longer whispered, it was suddenly whipping the tops of the swell into white spray. The Atlantic was stirring. Getting from the dinghy to the 'Sea Parrot' was not easy, but they were well-used to boats and got aboard without mishap, drawing the dinghy close on a short line. Gavin was priming the engine when Margaret caught sight of the other boat coming round the Knucklebones. He glanced up and saw the big black yawl rolling heavily at the point of the rocks. The engine of the

'Sea Parrot' coughed, died for an instant, then started. He went up into the bows.

"Half speed soon as the anchor's in and keep her into the sea." Margaret nodded, smiling happily. She loved handling their boat. As the anchor came in, the blunt bows drove slowly forward into a high green swell. Gavin tried to steady his glass on the other boat, but it was not easy for the 'Sea Parrot' rose and fell steeply below him. He made out three men: one in the yellow wheel-house, one clinging to the stumpy mast and a third with his head stuck out of the little hold. They were dressed in bright yellow oilskins.

"More speed," he shouted, "and turn towards them. Take it steady." The hull shuddered as the extra speed thrust the bows deeper into the sea; the old engine thudded and the first spray broke over the length of the deck.

"Steady, not so sharp. We'll roll to hell."

Gavin joined Margaret in the stern. Pusan stood in the bows, barking excitedly at the spray.

"I'll take her. Better put your coat on." The wind was much colder. Margaret shrugged herself into her short black oilskin. With her streaming, glistening face and excited eyes she looked about twelve years old.

"Those aren't fishermen." Gavin wiped the water from his eyes. "They don't look like bird-watchers either. Wave to them and see what happens."

She waved but the men did not answer.

"Can you make out the name?" He had to shout above the rising storm. Margaret tried unsuccessfully to steady the glass.

"No. Who'd be out on such an evening, in this sort of weather?"

He shook his head, glancing at the lowering sky and pursing his lips. Margaret patted the gunwale.

"She's a good boat."

A twenty-foot lobster boat, broad in the beam, solid as rock and gaily painted in red and black.

"It's the engine I'm not so sure of."

"We've got oars, and a sail." She smiled and shook the water from her soaking hair.

The yawl was heading straight for them, vanishing every now and then in a deeper trough, punching up sheets of spray.

"We don't want to pass inside her." Gavin changed course slightly. The other boat edged seawards.

"Nor do they."

The surf boiled among the black rocks of the Knucklebones and the thunder of the breaking seas was audible above the hard roar of the wind. By now the two boats were closing each other fast, rolling crabwise through the angry sea like two squat black animals. They could make out the men clinging to the wheel-house of the yawl quite clearly now. One of them put his head inside and seemed to be shouting to the man at the wheel. Then the first rain struck sharply at their faces, blurring their view. Gavin hung on to the bucking, bending tiller wondering how close he dared go. Astern of the 'Sea Parrot' the dinghy danced and plunged as though alive. About a hundred yards separated the boats, and still the yawl did not give way and make for open water. Gavin threw a quick glance at the Knucklebones. If they kept on this course they would be forced into the danger zone of those jagged rocks. If he turned seawards he would have to cut across the bows of the other boat and head into the seas risking a collision. Margaret was tense beside him, clinging tightly to the seat. He waved frantically. The men in the yawl made no sign in answer.

"God, they're mad! They'll have us on the rocks!" He yelled at the oncoming boat: "Get out of the way! Change course!"

The yawl plunged stubbornly towards them.

"Lifejackets! Quick! Get Pusan!"

Margaret got hold of the dog, gave Gavin the lifejacket and

put on her own. Gavin kicked off his heavy shoes. At fifty yards the two men vanished into the wheel-house. Gavin saw the dull gleams of the faces beyond the streaming glass. Then he felt the next sea lifting the boat towards the rocks. Another few yards and it would be too late.

"Hold on, I'm going to turn!" He opened the throttle wide and rammed hard at the tiller, praying for power. The 'Sea Parrot' met the seas head-on, slamming into the big waves so that she staggered astern from the blow. For a sickening moment the engine faltered, but it did not fail and she rose clear, sheering slowly away from the waiting rocks. If a big one came during the next few seconds they were over; nothing would save them. He wrestled with the tiller, heard his wife's cry of warning:

"Gavin, look out!"

The yawl had turned to follow course and was coming at their helpless rolling beam. He could do nothing. The boat, encumbered by the trailing dinghy, was turning sluggishly across the full weight of heavy seas. Again he waved his arm, gesticulating frantically. But the yawl held on her course.

"Jump when I shout!" He grabbed Margaret's arm, waiting for the moment. But the man at the other helm lost his nerve. He spun the wheel with all his strength, pulling his bows away from the 'Sea Parrot' so that for a moment the two boats lay on a parallel course with only a spitting distance of broken water between them. Gavin was cursing, fighting with the sea. Both boats were lifted high into the rain; the yawl was flung hard against the dinghy with a crash they could not hear.

"The axe! For God's sake! Cut the painter. Quick!"

Margaret grabbed the axe and severed the taut rope with two blows. Freed of the dead weight the 'Sea Parrot' lurched forward and clear of the yawl. At that moment the rain swept in sheets low over the water and blotted out the other boat.

"We'll have to make for the loch. We'd never reach Glenaila in this. She's making a lot of water. You'll have to bale." They rolled and plunged through the rain that hissed on darkening wastes of water.

"But what——?" Her words were whipped away by the wind. She began to bale. The boat reared suddenly like a frightened horse and then plunged downwards, pitching steeply on her nose. The screw jerked clear of the water, screaming. Gavin slackened speed just in time to save the shaft. The wind tore the crests of the waves to smoky shreds; great cold lumps of sea burst over the bows, smacking down on Margaret's bent back as she toiled with the baler. Poor Pusan crouched miserably in three inches of oily water. There was no longer any sign of the yawl; it had been swallowed in the dark murk of the storm. For by now it was blowing very hard and Gavin had no time to think of anything but how to keep the 'Sea Parrot' afloat and on course. Every sea threatened to capsize her or to throw her back, bows over stern; the wind tore viciously at their faces so that they gasped and could hardly breathe for the driving spray and rain.

But after a long haul they reached the partial shelter of the islands and the boat ceased to roll so violently. The waves gleamed in the darkness, trailing long white tails, but the uproar of the storm was slightly less and they no longer had to shout. Gavin saw the line of the surf along the Truina Sands.

"We ought to spot the lights of John's house." He leant forward and patted her shoulder. Her face turned to him, a pale blur through the rain. She smiled and returned to her task.

"Not much longer," he encouraged. "Then we'll be home and dry."

She climbed into the bows as he slowly put the helm over and headed into the mouth of the loch. The boat was lifted on a following sea and carried swiftly forward on the curling crest. He could just make out the figure of his wife and her frantically pointing arm. He held the tiller hard against the weight of the water; the next wave hurled them past the black teeth of the rocks, through milky surf. A touch, a graze and the bottom would be ripped out of her. Margaret's arm pointed again, stabbing to starboard. He felt the shaft shuddering as the screw came clear, but did not dare to slacken speed. A wall of dark water picked them up like a twig and swept them to safety in the comparative calm of the loch.

Gavin slowed the pounding engine and sat slumped, feeling slightly sick. His arms were quivering and the salt was sharp in his eyes. Margaret came to join him. He put his arms round her and felt the trembling of her body. Her hair was wet against his lips. He put the boat slowly towards the pier.

"You know how to handle a boat, Gavin," she said between chattering teeth. Now the danger was over she suddenly realised how bitterly cold she was, how very frightened she had been.

"I'd never have made it on my own. You were splendid, Margaret. Thank you." She brushed her cheek against his. "You're a good sort of woman to have about the place." From him that was compliment enough. A lantern bobbed on the pier.

The boat bumped against the sheltered stone. Thin rain swept across the light and the figure behind it.

"Finished with engines," said Gavin. Margaret nodded, too cold for speech.

"Is that yourself, Mr Blair? Och, get down with you, collie, you're wetter than a seal. I was seeing to the ponies and heard the boat—here, Mrs Blair, take my hand, right now, that's it. You'll be glad to be getting ashore. Man alive, but it's no sort of a night for boating."

* * * * *

Mrs Grant was a cosy white-haired little woman who even on tiptoe stood no higher than her husband's chest. She bustled about preparing a hot meal, clucking to herself like a worried hen. Margaret and Gavin sat close to the glowing peat fire warming the chill from their bodies. Her hair was very curly from the rain. Pusan lay in the heat, steaming gently.

"That's a terrible story you've been telling us, Mr Blair. But maybe there'll have been some mistake. The skipper was not seeing too well, or maybe he was drunk."

"They'll surely not have been trying to run you down." Mrs Grant shook her head in disbelief.

"That's what it looked like," said Margaret.

"It's not what it looked like, it's just exactly what they were doing. First they tried to push us on the rocks, then when that didn't work they tried to ram us."

The stalker took a long pull at his whisky, staring thoughtfully into the fire.

"Man alive, but that's a wicked thing to have done."

Mrs Grant clucked in agreement.

"What sort of a boat were you saying?"

"A yawl," said Margaret. "A big black yawl."

"It was not one of the East Coast boats?"

"No," answered Gavin, "not a ringer." Silence for a moment. The pleasant little hiss of the fire and the dull booming of the wind in the chimney, the chink of china as the final touches were put to the table.

"If it was the poachers," said Margaret doubtfully, "what were they doing out in daylight like that? Where had they been? What had they been doing?"

"Taking a spy at the ground, Mrs Blair. Looking for the deer. Or for a place to be landing some time."

"But how on earth could they have known it was us?"

"They'll maybe have watched you going out this morning. You have a boat that is easy to spot."

"Yes, but it still doesn't make sense," objected Gavin. "When they first saw us they could have altered course and passed well away from us. Instead they came absolutely bang straight for us."

"They were wanting to give you a wee bit of a fright," put in Mrs Grant.

Margaret laughed. "Well, they certainly succeeded. I've never been so terrified in all my life."

"Come away and have a bite to eat."

They sat at a table laden with oatcakes and scones; honey and butter and strawberry jam and homemade cake; there were grilled herrings and endless cups of strong sweet tea. For a while they munched in contented silence, till the stalker leant back in his chair and observed:

"These are dangerous men right enough. They have taken a shot at you——"

"And at Pusan." At the mention of his name the dog left the fire and came to sit by Margaret's side.

"Aye, Mrs Blair, and at the dog as well. And now they have come close to drowning you. These are not fellows to be played with." He took a gulp of tea. "They are telling you to keep your nose to yourself, Mr Blair. Aye, and it has been done before, many times. There is good money to be made in this business and they are not liking anyone to get in the way, not at all."

"D'you think they actually had deer with them?"

John Grant pulled slowly at his beard before answering. Gavin broke in:

"Not unless they got them last night or early this morning. All the deer are on the high ground at the moment. Isn't that right, John?"

"Aye. You'll not be finding deer on the shore after daybreak. That's the way the fisher lads take a beastie now and then, off the shore. So there's no reason why these fellows should not be playing the same game, none at all. But there are very few places a boat can be coming in to land and that might not be suiting such impatient rascals as these."

The storm snarled round the house, trembling the curtains and every now and then blowing a puff of peat-smell into the warm room. John Grant peered into his teacup, realising his dream in the dregs: to catch the little bastards red-handed and put bullets all round them, singing off the rocks and whumping into the peat-holes, scaring the hide off them, with maybe a wee flesh wound here and there. And these were worse than deer poachers; these were men who had gone close to murder.

"If they would be leaving the business to the stalkers and the ghillies I'm thinking they would not be coming back to take the deer in such a hurry," he growled. "And not a policeman would be needing to leave his fireside. Or the comfort of the public bar." He smiled in his beard. "Aye, we'd be taking care of them all right."

"Of course we would," echoed Margaret. "By the time we'd finished with them they wouldn't know if they were standing up or sitting down." She looked round the table. "Well, would they?"

The stalker allowed himself another of his rare smiles.

"Mrs Blair," he said slowly, "you could be having an army for the asking." If his look of admiration meant anything, John Grant would have marched at its head.

"The Fiery Cross," she said, her eyes dancing.

"Aye, I'm sometimes thinking that would not be such a bad idea at all," he answered seriously.

"We hadn't thought of that exactly," Gavin smiled. "But we are thinking of doing something on our own. Unofficially and without the blessed sanction of authority. In fact, we were discussing it with Captain Downie last night."

"And what was it you were thinking, Mr Blair?"

Gavin repeated the gist of their conversation. "When you really get down to it, I don't quite see what else we can do. Not unless we discovered where these men come from. Or managed to find out when they were going to appear next. Then we could be ready and waiting for them."

The stalker lit up his little black pipe: a sign of deep thinking. For a while he did not speak. Mrs Grant cleared the meal from the table and put more peat on the fire. Rain rattled on the windows. Margaret looked at her husband, shivered deliciously at the cosy warmth of the room and the sullen roar of the storm outside. They smiled at each other.

"You'll excuse me, Mr Blair, if I say that it would be better for you and the Captain to be getting on with your work and not wasting your time sitting on the Little Sister." The stalker spoke politely but firmly. Margaret saw the frown on Gavin's brow.

"John's right, darling," she said soothingly.

"But we want to catch these men, don't we?" His tone was faintly rebellious.

"Aye, Mr Blair, we do. And I am wanting to catch them as much as you are. This is my ground. This is where I have lived during all my life and——"

"I know, John. I'm sorry. I didn't mean that——"

"Do not be worrying yourself, Mr Blair. We are all anxious to get these fellows. But I am knowing every inch of Bealtuinn. I have watched for poachers for very many years. No, Mr Blair. I am the one to be doing the watching. You have your sheep. The winter is not so very far away and you will be busy."

Gavin sat downcast. Then he brightened. "You're quite right. But we'll come out with you whenever we've got the time."

"Another wee drop, Mr Blair? For the rotten night it is."

"That's very kind."

They discussed the matter amicably, with whisky in their glasses and the smoke billowing thicker and thicker from the pipe. Grant would talk to Duncan and Finlay and old Donald Macrae out at Glen Eishie. They might be hearing things that the police would never be knowing about, not if they lived to be a hundred and fifty. They and the shepherds and the ghillies. Some of those lads had their ears close to the ground right enough. He would maybe have a word with that old scoundrel, Aeneas Macdonald, who had been dealing in poached game ever since he was a boy.

"If none of them can be helping—well, they'll not be the men I am thinking they are."

So they left it at that. Secretly Gavin was relieved. There was a great deal to be done before the coming of the first snows. God knows if he'd manage it on his own.

The stalker told one or two of his favourite stories, mostly of his years in the trenches; he told them well, with all the story-telling genius of the Highlander. It was warm and hospitable and altogether delightful sitting by the fire, listening with half an ear to the anger of the wind and rain, and they were loath to leave. It was Margaret who noticed the clock.

"Oh, Gavin, look at the time. We *must* go. It's almost half-past eleven. Poor Chiquita, she'll be absolutely starving."

"And how is the wee thing?" Mrs Grant paused from her knitting.

"Thriving and terribly spoilt."

The stalker tapped out his pipe, emptied his glass. "I'll be getting out the old car."

"Certainly not," said Margaret. "We can walk back by the sea. Can't we, darling?"

Gavin did not answer. Her sense of distance wasn't all that good at times.

"No, John, of course we can walk."

"You walk, my dear. I'll expect you home by about half-past two," Gavin chuckled.

"Nobody will be walking, Mrs Blair. Not on a night like this. And not by the Quaking Sands."

They drove in his rickety little car in which the stalker had to sit bent like some giant gnome with his beard jutting to the windscreen. The lights were dim through the pelting rain and the wind buffeted the car fiercely, swerving it into the pot-holes. Beyond Hump Bridge the storm howled up the Glen of the Skull, driving curtains of rain across their path. The car swayed violently.

"Man alive, but what was that?" A pile of stones loomed close in front. He wrenched at the wheel and they went bumping by. "Those damned county council fellows, putting their silly wee stones in the middle of the road and not in the holes where they belong." The stalker swore angrily under his breath. The wheels bounced sickeningly in and out of a dozen craters before anyone ventured to speak.

"I see they've moved Finlayson off this bit," said Gavin loudly, above the shindy of the engine.

"Yes, and put such an odd-looking creature in his place." Margaret leant forward with her face between the heads of the two men. "With a droopy moustache and the most enormous bat ears. It's a shame. Finlayson was so nice."

"That sounds like Jimmy Robertson. Had he a crooked nose, Mrs Blair? A nose to see round corners?"

"Yes—yes, I think he had."

"Aye, that'll be Jimmy right enough."

"Wasn't he at Famista once, a long time ago, when the Mackenzies were living there?"

"He was stalker at Famista until he was getting his notice from Colonel Mackenzie." He negotiated the bridge over the Black Burn. "James Robertson was a man deeply devoted to the bottle. After his wife died he was never on the hill, never at all. There wasn't a decent stag left on the whole of Famista, not from the river to the lochs. Och, the poaching boys got him blazing drunk that often he couldn't tell sunrise from sunset." Grant uttered one of his rare laughs. "One time they took him back to his bed. 'Goodnight, Jimmy,' they were saying, and then off for his boat to go poaching salmon."

As the car rounded the great mass of Beinn Mhor the storm lifted, the rain slackened and the darkness lightened appreciably. A few stars were visible among ragged, flying clouds.

"They say he went to Stornoway for a time and got mixed

up in something very unlawful. So now he's back again and working on the roads. Well, well, I did not know."

Passing the Wailing Loch, the stalker was still muttering to himself: "Jimmy Robertson. Well, well."

Gavin glanced sideways at his wife and saw the quick gleam of her smile. He suddenly felt immensely tired. He longed to be safely in bed with her lying close beside him and all the cares and worries of the world banished by her soft arms.

It was then that he looked ahead and saw the sheep lying in the road between the white gates of his home.

[6]

THE ram was dead, its throat cut, lying in a pool of black blood; rain glistened in the staring white eye. Gavin straightened up. He did not say anything but stood looking down at the dead animal, his hands clenched into hard fists. Margaret, who had been standing beside him, gave a sudden cry and began to run towards the house. He and John pulled the ram clear of the road. It was raining again and the curly horns were slippery in their hands.

"So that's what the little bastards were doing." The stalker swore as he watched Gavin disappear into the rain after his wife. Then he drove slowly to the house. A torch was flashing by the open byre door and he found the two of them, with Mrs Blair calling for the calf.

Gavin played the beam round the whitewashed interior. The little straw bed lay scattered all over the place. The calf had gone. Margaret was distraught.

"They've killed her, oh, Gavin, I know they've killed her." He tried to comfort her but she hardly listened. "I'm going to look for her."

"Not in this, Margaret. It's useless, you'd never see a yard."

The wind was swirling the rain round the corner of the building and the night had gone as black as the pit, thick with sand and spindrift. The crash and boom of the sea made normal speech impossible and they had to shout.

"You'd best be waiting, Mrs Blair."

"Wait!" she cried. "Can't you understand? She may be hurt. She may be lying out there bleeding to death. We can't wait." She snatched the torch from Gavin's hand and ran into the lashing night.

"Margaret, come back!" But she had gone.

"John, find her. I'll get the lantern."

Gavin went with his lantern through the storm and found them down at the bottom of the sea-meadow, near the fence. Margaret was on her knees beside the other ram. It lay on its side and the rain thinned the blood which ran from the cruelly beaten head. In the flickering glare of the lantern they saw the wild rolling of its eye and the gaping wound along its foreleg. Between them they half dragged, half carried the dying ram up to the byre and laid it gently in the straw where Chiquita had slept. Gavin inspected the brutal wounds about the skull and neck. He glanced at the stalker, who shook his head slowly. Margaret sat down and took the battered head in her lap, soothing as a woman would soothe a sick child. The dying animal seemed to understand, for it tried to raise itself and look at her, but the effort was too great and fresh blood gushed from its open mouth. John Grant stood above them, turning a bloodstained spade over and over in his hands.

"This is what they were using. Man alive, but they are cruel, filthy devils."

"Who could do a thing like this? *Who?*" Margaret wiped the red froth from the ram's nostrils. The final struggle for life began; the hooves clattered on the cobblestones; the neck stretched agonisingly and the head jerked, flicking blood over her clothes. Once, twice it snorted, then, quivering, it stiffened and died. Margaret sat with the tears running down her face, one small hand still clenched tightly in the depths of the reddened wool.

"Oh, Gavin, Gavin." He went down beside her, murmuring encouragement and kissing the tears from her skin. The stalker went to the door and stood looking out into the rain lancing across the light from the door. He was once again cursing to himself, fluently in his own tongue.

Margaret leant against her husband for a moment's comfort, then, pushing him gently away, she got to her feet.

"I'm all right now. I'm sorry, darling." She was calm but very pale, the tears glistening on her white skin.

"Now we must find Chiquita," she said in a flat, hard voice. They followed her outside and searched in the rain, probing hopelessly with the torch and the lantern into the black storm; calling hopelessly against the huge sound of the sea. They found that the gate to the beach was open, swinging in the wind. Margaret cupped her hands to her mouth.

"I'll go as far as the point." A few steps and she had gone from view, blotted out by the rain and spray.

"For God's sake, be careful," he called, but the words were whipped from his lips, away like flying leaves. He knew she would never give up, not if she had to search all night.

"You'll want to be getting back," he shouted to the stalker. "It's damned late."

"And leave you and Mrs Blair?" A big sea broke on the rocks and they ducked from the sheets of spray. Gavin heard a faint cry through the storm.

"She's calling. Come on."

They made their way along the beach, shielding their faces from the sting of the sand.

"There it is again." He heard her voice calling for him. Grant heard nothing but the thunder of the sea. Gavin yelled in answer, suddenly very frightened. If she'd gone too far out on the rocks in this and slipped—— "Margaret, where are you? I'm here, Margaret, I'm here!"

With one last frenzied roar the squall rushed away, clearing the night so that he saw her coming towards them. In her arms she was carrying the sodden and utterly terrified calf. Gavin made to take the little animal but Margaret shook her head. They returned to the house.

"It was her bell," said Margaret. "I heard it tinkling and found her stuck on a spit of sand almost surrounded by water. Another few minutes and she'd have been swept away. Oh, thank goodness we got her that bell!" Chiquita lay before the fire as Pusan had done, wrapped in a towel with only her head showing.

"They must have opened the door and she ran out. Think, Gavin, if they'd found her they'd have killed her, wouldn't they?"

"Very likely, yes."

The death of his rams had filled him with a cold vicious anger and he sat frowning into the flames. Now and then he struck his thigh with clenched fist. Margaret came to sit by him, her head on his knee. Absently he stroked her soft, drying hair.

"What are we going to do?" she asked.

"Tell Donald first thing in the morning. Not that he can do much, lying in bed with 'flu. Bury the tups. Think about getting some new ones."

"But won't the police want to see them?"

"Will they? Yes, I suppose they will. I don't know. I'm not thinking very straight. God, what a bloody thing to do!"

Margaret rubbed her cheek gently against his hand. "I know, darling. But we've got to think about what to do, how to catch these brutes. It's no use brooding, Gavin. That won't bring the rams back."

"I know. Tomorrow. After some sleep." His head ached, he felt utterly exhausted and dispirited. If he'd been alone he'd have very likely got himself extremely drunk.

"Wasn't John angelic?" she said, trying to change the subject.

"Yes."

The stalker had stayed for a while before departing for Bealtuinn. "I'll not be wanting Mrs Grant to be worrying herself. She'll be thinking the car has dropped to pieces under me. Och, no, Mrs Blair, it's many a time I've been a sight wetter than this on the hill. You'll be letting me know what happens, Mr Blair, and what Donald is saying about the matter." He had paused, half in and half out of his car. "And if there is anything any of us in Bealtuinn can be doing to help at all, you'll be letting us know."

"Bed, darling. Come along. It's no good sitting there getting yourself more upset."

In bed he lay with his aching head in the softness of her shoulder and at once felt relief. "We'll tell Donald and Mike," he whispered, "but no one else. We don't want the whole place yapping their heads off. Though they're pretty well bound to find out I suppose. Everyone always knows everything. Usually before it's happened." The wind rushed against the house, spattering thin rain on the windows.

"But *why*, Gavin? *Why?*"

"To make me mind my own business. It's happened before. People have had their stacks burned and fences torn down. These sort of men don't play according to the rules. They're in it for big money and to hell with anyone who gets in the way."

"But you haven't got in the way."

"They didn't like being hit and they didn't like having bits taken out of them by dogs with sharp teeth. Nor did they like leaving the deer behind. Oh, yes, I got in the way all right."

"What I can't make out is how did they know it was you? I mean, each time it's been dark. How do they know it wasn't Mike? Or John? Or somebody's shepherd?"

"Don't forget they had a good look at the car that first time."

"What it really boils down to is that they've got someone local helping them. Someone who knows your car. He may even know Pusan. It was moonlight after all." They lay considering this.

"Yes," said Gavin. "Yes, I think you may've got something, love. We'll see what Donald has to say. And Marr. There's a chap with his head screwed on all right. If anyone's going to get anything done, then it's him."

"None of this will bring back Simon and Peter," she said sadly.

"No, but it may help to get the men who killed them." He turned his head and kissed her neck. "We'll get them, Margaret. Somehow, between us all, we'll get them. We must. We damned well must."

The sea crashed and thundered on the shore and the squally wind tore noisily round their house as they lay and whispered together. Just before they fell asleep, Gavin said: "I think we'll go into Fort Henry tomorrow. I'll go and see Marr. I expect you've got things to do. Then we'll have lunch and perhaps go to a film. Do us good."

* * * * *

Except for two shrill girls in twin-sets and tweed skirts, and a silent trio of gloomy-faced commercials, Gavin and Margaret had the hotel dining-room to themselves. They drank their watery fruit juice and he told her about his interview with Inspector Marr.

"As usual there wasn't much he could say, because as usual there wasn't much to go on. A black fishing boat tries to sink us——"

"Did you tell him it had a canary wheel-house?"

"Yes. He jotted it down. In fact, he jotted it all down. The two tups being killed. There at least is something definite, except, of course, they couldn't tell us who killed them. He asked strings of questions, quick-fire stuff like a policeman in a film, and got slightly stuffy over the fact I hadn't reported the whole thing to Donald last night."

"Last night? What could he possibly have done last night?"

"That's what I said."

"In the middle of a howling storm. Why, he couldn't even have made the wheels of his bicycle go round in that wind." They laughed. "Even if he hadn't been lying in bed."

"I know. I told him. He wasn't best pleased about that

either. Anyway, he's coming out himself some time tomorrow morning, so Simon and Peter will just have to stay unburied till he's been. By the way, I asked him to lunch, if that's all right. He wants a general snoop round, as he put it."

They ordered roast beef and Yorkshire pudding from a pert waitress with mauve lipstick and badly camouflaged spots.

"Oh, and a pint of draught, please. Or shall we be devils and have wine?"

"We haven't really very much to celebrate, have we, darling?"

"All the more reason."

An elderly waiter brought the wine list. One of the shrill girls smiled toothily at Margaret who waved, smiling and saying from the corner of her mouth: "It's that rather fearful Buckham-Knocker girl. You remember, the one at the Philpotts' party, the one who cornered us and screamed about modern art. But what else did he say, Gavin? I mean, are they actually *doing* anything?"

"I've no doubt that behind the scenes the wheels of the law are grinding away in their own slow, conscientious way. Though it's difficult to see what they've got to go on. Oh, the boat, yes. But what happens? Inquiries are made and the skipper says he was in port or fishing off the Faroes on the day and date in question. *We* know who killed the tups, but that, as the Inspector pointed out, is not proof."

The beef arrived, tough and gristly, accompanied by soggy lumps of blackened batter. They munched in silence. In common with most eating-places in Britain the room was silent and oppressive, disturbed only by the clatter of cutlery and muted furtive bursts of talk from the commercial table. Even the two girls were overcome by the atmosphere. Soon they paid and left. On her way out the girl Buckham-Knocker stopped at their table and gushed, all teeth and superlatives. Gavin rose to his feet politely. Margaret switched on her social face.

"*Do* tell," shrilled Buckham-Knocker. "It *was* you, wasn't it, who had that dreadful experience with the poachers the other night? How too *shattering*. Margaret, you must have been quite *frantic*." On she waffled. 'Richard was saying the other night at dinner, of course it's all that perfectly ridiculous Sheriff Whinnie." She threw a quick look at the commercials, and leant closer. "Of course you know what Flavia said, quite seriously too—that he gets a rake-off every time he lets them go with a tiny fine." She giggled. "You know what Flavia is, she says anything, simply *anything*, to make an effect. Of course, he's completely on the poachers' side, we all know that. Daddo calls him the Poachers' Friend. You know, like the Prisoner's Friend in the Navy. If you ask me, the man's an absolute *red*."

Gavin crumbled his bread. Margaret smiled sweetly and encouragingly.

"Tony had an extraordinary theory—oh, but you must know Tony surely, Tony D'Erlanger, *such* a charmer, we were all dining at the Mackenzies' two nights ago. My *dear*, have you been there since they did up the house? I don't want to sound catty or anything, but really——"

"Do tell us about Mr—er—Tony—his theory."

"*Well*, he said these perfectly dreadful people, the poachers, probably had some sort of central hiding-place where they brought the poor creatures, the deer, before distributing them to all the butchers and things. Somewhere tucked away, all cosy-cosy, deep in some glen or other, miles from anywhere, madly John Buchanish and exciting. Daddo thinks there may only be two or three gangs in the whole of Scotland, nipping about all over the place in vans and lorries and things."

"Controlled by some master mind?" Gavin looked up at her jolly, flushed face.

"Oh, do you think so?"

"Sheriff Whinnie perhaps?"

She neighed loudly. "Oh, how too priceless! I must tell Mumsie, she'll absolutely adore it. Of course, Daddo says a good deal of the blame should be on the absentee lairds. He says if they weren't always away in their breweries or paper-mills or fiddling about on the Stock Exchange or somewhere, or sunning themselves in the West Indies, and spent a bit more time up here getting things properly organised, there wouldn't be *half* this dreadful poaching."

"He's got something there," Gavin said.

"What is it the Socialists are always saying?" Margaret asked.

Gavin laughed. "Big Business Lairds, in capital letters, treat their vast Highland acres as sporting playgrounds for themselves and their stinking rich friends. A good line. Sometimes pretty hard to argue against."

"I *knów*," agreed Buckham-Knocker. "Such *wonderful* ammunition for them, isn't it? Goodness, I must fly. Marjorie's making the most absurd faces to come on. When are you coming to see us? Yes, you *must*. Daddo's longing to hear all about your adventure. Dinner one night, *very* soon. I'll get Mumsie to ask the Farquharsons. She's *sò* amusing. Then you can simply *rivet* us all with your flirt with danger. We're all simply dying to hear it first-hand. Oh, dear, poor Marjorie. 'Bye now." She tore from the room.

"Well," said Gavin, "they certainly make them all shapes and sizes. Phew!"

"She's really not so bad, darling. Just an overdose of youth, that's all." They finished their wine.

"That chap she was talking about, Derringer or Dullinger or —yes, well him, anyway—there might be something in that idea. Of a hideout somewhere. A place to park the stuff and to keep the vehicle and the weapons. Where they can get themselves sorted out and plan the next operation."

"They may be sitting there at this very minute deciding

where to go next. It's horrible, darling. And as far as I can see there's nothing, absolutely nothing, we can do about it."

"This place, if it exists, could be anywhere within a radius of—well, it might be ten miles, or it might be fifty. For all we know it could be a perfectly respectable farm somewhere. Talk about needles. No, the only hope is to get them if they come back. Of course, the police might happen to stumble on something via the local grapevine. Things get about in an uncanny sort of way in these parts. But there's really not much point in us trying to turn ourselves into amateur bloodhounds. You don't agree, darling, do you? You've got your stubborn face on. You want to go tearing about tracking them down. You'd like to surround their hideout and burst in shouting 'Hands up', and find them thumbing through wads of fivers, surrounded by poached deer and empty cartridge cases."

"Now you're laughing at me."

"Never."

Presently they went next door for their coffee. The room was empty save for a figure hidden behind a copy of the local paper. They sipped their hot and fairly nasty coffee in front of a large hissing fire.

"It'll be all over the countryside that Sheriff Whinnie is the leader of a dozen poaching gangs—oh yes, Gavin Blair was telling us the other day." She threw back her head, draining her cup and crunching the sugar between her little white teeth. Gavin shook his head warningly, glancing at the raised paper. She smiled at him mischievously. "Daddo and Mumsie will enjoy the idea, anyway."

A gust of wind rattled the big window overlooking the square. Gavin yawned and stretched his arms above his head. "I suppose we'll have to be starting back before it gets any worse."

During the night the rain had hardened to sleet, and since they had been in Fort Henry to scattered snow-showers. Already the mountains rising beyond the rooftops were smothered in heavy grey cloud; people in the square made sudden swift clutches at their hats, and their faces were pinched and blue. A few snowflakes danced across the window-panes, staring now and then against the warmer glass in melting beauty. Margaret scooped up the last of the crunchy sugar.

"We don't particularly want to be stranded. Besides, think of the animals."

"Think of the seats more like." They had left Pusan and the calf Chiquita curled up side by side on the back seat. "A lot can happen in three hours."

"Lots. But we couldn't have left them at home."

He got up and went to the window. The snow was thickening; by now it was difficult to make out the opposite side of the square, and the mountains had quite vanished. The few cars parked outside the hotel were white-roofed. As he watched idly a van drove into the square and stopped. The windscreen was white and brown snow was caked solid below the mudguards. Two men tumbled out of the back, beating their arms and stamping their feet even though dressed in scarves and balaclava helmets and bulky duffel jackets. They began to strap chains to the rear wheels, stopping every now and then to blow on their fingers. The job was obviously not to their liking. He could see their angry expressions and gestures.

"Not much cop on a day like this," remarked a voice. The other occupant had left his paper and stood beside him looking down at the struggling men. "Too cold by half," he added.

Gavin agreed.

"By the way," went on the stranger, "I wonder if you've got the right time on you?"

Gavin told him. He was a stocky youngish man, about forty or thereabouts with very thick blond hair and the palest of blue eyes. Paler even than Kenny's. Cruel eyes, Gavin thought, yet they lit up pleasantly enough as the man smiled and said:

"I'd give a good deal to be staying in here by this fire."

"Are you going far?" Margaret asked politely.

He turned to face her. "For my sins, yes, much too far." He gave her a little half nod, half bow. He laughed. But this time the eyes did not light up. He wore the tie of a very large and famous public school and spoke like it. "It's getting pretty thick. Still, with luck, it may only be showers." With another of his little bows to Margaret he strode quickly from the room.

"We're meeting all the gentry and quality today," she said. "I wonder who that was."

"No idea."

For some reason Gavin had not taken to the man. Perhaps it had been those cold eyes. He rang for the bill and returned to his watch at the window. Margaret joined him, and together they watched the men putting on the last chain. The blond man came out of the hotel, pulling on a short thick jacket like those worn by telephone linesmen. He scorned a cap. For a moment he hesitated, glancing right and left, then, seeming suddenly to make up his mind, he walked briskly towards the van. As he came level with the men he stopped and said something. One of the men looked up and nodded. Then the blond man continued on his way, out of the square, taking the Bealtuinn road.

"I wonder where he's off to, so spry and confident?" she mused.

"Probably left his car at the station garage, I don't know."

Gavin was paying for the coffee when he heard a sharp exclamation from the window.

"Gavin, quick. Look, isn't that the man who works on the roads? Jimmy Something-or-Other? The one John was talking about?"

"Robertson. Yes, that's him all right. I'd know that moustache anywhere."

The man stood, hunched deep inside his turned-up collar by

the tobacconist's on the corner, then he slouched slowly across to the van with his hands in his pockets. He stood watching the men as they completed the job and straightened up.

"Goodness, darling, he's getting in with them."

The driver got out, cleared the windscreen, jumped back in and the van moved off through the snow, also taking the road for Bealtuinn.

"Well," said Margaret wonderingly, "what d'you make of that little drama?"

In answer Gavin seized her arm. "Get your coat and come on. I'll be in the car. Hurry."

The engine was cold and stiff, the battery weak; he had to use the handle. "Hop in and give her a bit of choke. More. A bit more. Not so much. That's it. Accelerator. Not too hard. Damn!" The engine died.

An hour later they took the road for Bealtuinn. Gavin was covered with oil and in a filthy temper. He drove very fast, to the utmost capacity of the old engine, leaning forward, peering through the snow, his face close to the glass. He said nothing. She said nothing but just hung on, supposing he knew what he was doing. The back-end of the car waggled like a fishtail on the sharp bends.

"It's them," he said suddenly. "I'm damned sure it is. The van, three men, four with Robertson. An evening when the roads'll be deserted and everyone indoors. No visibility. The deer low down, close to the road. It all adds up. Donald in bed, oh yes, it all fits. There's your local contact, Margaret—that chap Robertson. Ex-stalker. Knows the ground, knows the deer. A man with a grudge, and a drunkard on top of it. By God, wait till John hears about this!"

He switched on the headlights. The tracks of chains were still easily visible.

"Once we get to the fork we'll see which way they're going in. My bet's Hump Bridge."

Margaret turned to soothe the restive calf.

"Darling?"

"Mm."

"Have you thought what we're going to do if it *is* the poachers and we *do* catch up with them?"

"Not exactly, no. Have you?"

"No."

He was seized by a sudden nasty spasm of doubt. His foot eased slightly off the accelerator. They were a ruthless bunch who'd play pretty rough if cornered, and the mere fact of her being a woman wouldn't cut much ice. He couldn't risk her getting hurt, not to catch all the poachers in the world. He slowed even more. What the hell *could* they do? There were four men in the van, almost certainly armed, and one at least among them perfectly ready to use his weapon. Well, they couldn't stop now, that was certain.

Snowflakes came dancing at the car, uprushing before they struck the glass. The mountains were visible now and then, dark and hugely menacing on each side of the road.

"This is the real stuff," said Gavin. These were not fat wet flakes to melt as they touched ground; this was snow to lie, to drift, to turn killer when driven by an icy wind.

Margaret shivered. "Ugh, I hate it."

"They're taking a hell of a chance coming in on a night like this. If it drifts, then they've had it."

"We don't know it's the poachers, do we? I mean, it may be some perfectly harmless friends of Kenny's or Donald's."

He did not answer, holding the car steady in another savage gust. The little warm windows of isolated crofts came and went; sheep showed white in the lights and the telegraph wires flowed jerkily by, bright steel threads; the dark ranks of a small pine wood, quickly left behind, Margaret sat very quiet. Once she spoke gently to the animals; once she put her hand briefly on Gavin's arm. The driving snow was blanketing the headlights and their speed dropped to a crawl. It was almost impossible to make out the marks of the chains.

At the fork Gavin stopped and got out.

"Hump Bridge. It's them all right." He thought for a second or two, then took the road to Rappoch. "We'll pick up Kenny and leave word at Donald's." He increased speed. "Hold tight, darling, and pray for the dawn." The car bounced and bucketed through a succession of worsening snow-showers.

At the policeman's house Margaret ran in. She returned panting. "Not much help. Mrs Donald tried to ring Fort Henry but nothing happened, the line must be down already."

"Hell!"

They had no luck at Kenny's. The shop was shut and his mother had no idea where he could be. No, she was sorry but he had gone out some while back. So that was that, they were on their own.

"What about Mike?" suggested Margaret.

"Not time. Willing to take a chance? Just the two of us?"

She nodded. "We've got to go past the bridge, anyway, darling, to get home," she answered bravely.

[7]

THE night had cleared and quietened for a spell and the mountains rose white on their left; on the right the river was a black tumbling serpent between the snow-covered banks. Gavin stopped the car below Sgurr Gheal, switched off and listened, but they could only hear the rush of the river. Very slowly they crept forward without lights. Pusan stood with his front paws on Margaret's shoulders whining his excitement. With a roar another snow-storm swept up the Stag Burn, half blinding them.

"There's a light at the bridge," cried Margaret. "I'm sure I saw it."

Gavin saw it too: the pinpoint flash of a torch. "Hang on tight, we'll have to rush them!"

He put the car at the bridge, giving her all she'd take, switching on the headlights. The car slithered all over the road with tyres howling. The parapets of the bridge loomed very close through the slackening snow. A figure leapt wildly out of the way waving its arms. They saw a car tilted on its side in the ditch, almost hit it, then they were through, snaking and swerving half out of control.

"Stop, Gavin. You must stop. That was the Minister."

The car slammed to a slithering stop.

"The Minister? Can't have been."

But it was. And in a high state of excitement too.

"Thank the Lord, Mr Blair. I was thinking I was here all night. I——"

"Have you seen a van?" Gavin broke in.

"A van, Mr Blair? Yes, indeed I have seen a van. It put me into the ditch. Driving without lights at a hundred miles an hour. They were over the bridge and on me so quick I only just had time to swerve out of the way. Another foot or so and we'd have met head-on. Surely it was a madman driving——"

Gavin interrupted again. "Which way?"

The Minister pointed towards Glenaila. "They are not friends of yours?"

"Poachers. Deer poachers."

"Poachers! So those are the scoundrels who——" The Minister was fated not to be allowed to finish a sentence.

"How long ago?"

"An hour. Maybe more."

"You must be frozen," said Margaret. "Get in at once and keep warm."

The Minister brushed snow from his long black overcoat and his tweed hat. His glasses were blurred by melting snow. He got in, sputtering with indignation and blowing on his mittened hands.

"Providence sent you, Mrs Blair."

"We followed them from Fort Henry," said Gavin tersely. "Now we've got to think what to do next."

"If I could be getting my hands on the scoundrels." The Reverend Andrew Sinclair blew on his fingers. If he had gone to war the Minister would undoubtedly have been one of those splendid militant padres longing secretly to carry an offensive weapon with which personally to strike down God's enemies.

"First of all, is your car completely stuck?"

"I fear so. Too much for us to manage. I'll be needing a tow."

"Pity. We could have blocked the road with her. If the van's gone this way, then it's got to come back this way. There's no other road."

"Then we have them," rejoiced the Minister. "We have them in a trap."

"Yes. But they're like rats these men, very dangerous in traps. Right, Minister, your car's out so we'll have to use this one. And the best place for a road-block is the Black Burn bridge."

They drove the half-mile through another swirling shower, following the tracks of the van. At the bridge Gavin slewed the car across the road, blocking the retreat from Glenaila.

"If they are driving in the same reckless way," said the Minister doubtfully, "they will certainly run into your car."

"That'll be just too bad. She's past her best, anyway. We'll get into the trees and see what happens."

Between the road and the river there was a small clump of broken skeleton fir trees, reaching almost to the road edge.

"Shouldn't one of us be going for assistance?" suggested the Minister.

"Never make it in time. John Grant's the nearest and he's a good two miles. Damn, if only we had your car." Gavin looked at the Reverend Sinclair. He was not an old man and was heftily built. "You may get your chance at these brutes yet."

The Minister smiled. "We're outnumbered, so our only hope is surprise. We'll have to prevent them from getting out of the van." There was a tyre-lever in the car and the starting-handle, and a walking stick for Margaret. "Keep them cooped up inside and we're all right. When they try to get out, hit them—and hit them hard." The Minister tried a few sweeping blows with the tyre-lever.

They got into the shelter of the trees. Margaret tied Chiquita to one swaying trunk, Pusan to another. "No, Gavin, he's staying here, he's not going to be shot again."

They did not have long to wait. An automatic weapon opened fire below Beinn Mhor; long, sustained bursts, from not too far away.

"I'm going up there to have a look. Stay here, Margaret, and you, Minister. If the van turns up, don't let it get past. If I can get in among them it may upset their plan and save a few deer."

"Darling, be careful!"

But he was gone. The Minister hesitated, not knowing what to do.

"You must go with him—please."

"But—no, Mrs Blair. I cannot be leaving you here alone."

They heard another burst of fire, muffled by the snow, then nothing but the sounds of the river and wind in the trees.

* * * * *

Long before it came, the deer of Bealtuinn had sensed the approach of the storm; they smelt it perhaps or maybe they even heard it forming in the yellowish northern clouds. Whatever the answer they began to move down from the high ground; in small parties they came, unhurried yet purposeful. Now and then they stopped to feed, throwing up their heads ever more frequently as they moved towards danger. Ten hours after they had begun to move the rain of the lowlands was sweeping across the heights as sleety snow.

The thin white skin covered the rocks, clung to the frozen grass and to the staring coat of the big black stag. He moved slowly, exhausted by his weeks of sexual indulgence; his body was worn to a skeleton by the rut and his great head when it came up to sniff the breezes seemed ungainly and top-heavy. Except for a few ptarmigan croaking and ruffling, he was alone on the long bare ridge of Creag Dhu. But when the wind came, lifting the frozen snow into fine spume so that every rock trailed a little white tail, then the stag made his way to his usual sanctuary above the Cave of the Laughing Men.

By morning, at the time when Gavin was digging the graves for his slaughtered sheep, the mountains were well covered, swept bare in patches here and there where the snow had been whirled away by the ravening wind. The leaden clouds dropped low over the snowfields, and only the crouching ptarmigan and some whitening mountain hares remained above two thousand feet to challenge the white wilderness.

The black stag remained in shelter till the early afternoon, then, at the approach of dusk, made his way down into the Glen of the Skull. Near the Black Burn he came upon other deer and caught, as they did, the first scent of man. They were bunched fearfully on the flat ground, sensing danger but having no idea from where it might come. A hind made a sudden little rush, the others following, to cluster in fresh panic, peering this way, that way, into the gathering darkness. The stag kept clear, for in the face of danger his instinct was to be alone and not hemmed-in by a mass of frightened animals. He followed along the deer path, stepping slowly and often raising his muzzle to the wind. In the corries and ravines the winds can play impish tricks and those who set out to stalk and kill the red deer must know these tricks or they will not get within a mile of their quarry. So now a flurry of wind swooping round the shoulder of Beinn Mhor brought as well as snow the fresh warning of man. The stag sheered away down the path towards the sea and as he did so the snow lifted.

The Glen of the Skull was filled with deer; there must have been fully six hundred moving towards the entrance to the Chasm in a jostling shadowy mass. But when the leaders heard the shot in front of them they stopped, while those at the far back still pressed forward. The deer in front stood irresolute and terrified, stamping their feet, not knowing whether to rush forward and make for the sea or to turn back. The wind dropped, and in the silence an old hind barked and at once was answered by a second shot, the clapping of hands and loud shouts.

At that the deer broke and stampeded, some back up the slopes of Creag Dhu, others stretched their necks and made for the sea. To the men posted at the entrance to the Chasm the sound of their running was like a charge of cavalry, drumming on the hard ground, clattering on the rocks. The greater part of the herd had turned and were making back up the Glen towards Beinn Mhor—as they were meant to; hinds and calves and young staggies led by an old grey hind of much experience. With them, in the air above their open panting mouths and staring eyes, travelled the ugly smell of fear.

Two men stood at the end of the Chasm track where it joined the path running through Skull Glen. One of them laughed.

"No need to 'ang about 'ere any more. It's too perishin' cold. We've done our bit." He slung his rifle on his shoulder.

"Cor, wrap up. It's enough to freeze a muckin' brass monkey."

"Aye," muttered his companion, "those deer will not be stopping now, not before they reach the road."

"Not before they reach the others, you mean."

James Robertson led them back along the path in the tracks of the fleeing deer. He wanted to get away, out of the Glen of the Skull. Only money had brought him there at all—a lot of money. Only money brought him to kill the deer in this barbarous way.

"The others'll fix 'em."

Robertson grunted and went faster.

"Christ, this trip ought to pay us o.k." The words were drowned by the rushing roar of the waterfall. They went past the big rowan tree and across the stepping-stones and away from the noise of the burn. Robertson was waiting for the shots. Any moment now. The deer were running fast, straight for the other men, and if the snow kept off they'd be getting them point-blank. A tommy gun and a rifle at that range—aye, there'd be a big killing right enough, with the beasts showing against the snow.

Away in front, the deer were running sure-footed over the broken ground, and with them ran the black stag, carried along like a broken stick on the current, unable to break clear, trapped by the tide of panting, bumping bodies. Beside him a small calf kept up desperately on its little legs, bleating with the fear of losing its mother. The night was alive with the sounds of distress, the scrabble of hooves on rock, the thud of pounding feet.

A new sound smashed into the darkness: the stammering clatter of automatic fire, and with it the *thump* and *thwack* of heavy bullets in living flesh. The maddened animals tried vainly to scatter, to increase their speed, to break away from death. But their numbers impeded them and they milled frantically, the living and the wounded and the dead. Stabs of bright flame lit the muzzles of the two weapons jerking at the dark mass of struggling deer. Bullets tore into shoulders, stomachs and sometimes, mercifully, into heads; they flattened hideously on bone, drilled neatly through flesh; they shattered legs and jaws and went singing from the rocks.

And in the shadows the two butchers laughed and shouted with the crazed fever of the killing.

The black stag had stopped short of the lethal zone. He fought his way clear of the panic and ran for the safety of Creag Dhu. Close at his heels, bursting its small heart to keep up, toiled the calf. Snow sprayed from their hooves and a gust of clean wind blew away the horrid stench of men and powder and blood. After a while the stag slowed his pace to a walk, allowing the little animal to catch up. It trotted bravely on, sticking very close to the stag. Flecks of foam hung from the corners of its open mouth; the tongue lolled out and the small head drooped with exhaustion. Threads of blood trickled down one flank from a furrow ploughed across its back. They heard running human feet, and the man-smell was strong in their nostrils. The black stag and his little companion sprang forward into the shelter and safety of freshly falling snow.

* * * * *

Gavin caught a vague glimpse of the calf as it ran by. But the shape was quickly swallowed by the shower which had blotted out Beinn Mhor. Looking back he could no longer see the road. He thought he heard a voice that might have been calling his name. Then a rifle fired three shots in quick succession. He made for the sound, stumbling in the drifted snow. More deer went past him, heading back for the road; a hind staggered out of the swirling murk to fall almost at his feet. Blood pumped into the snow from a shocking wound in her neck. He stayed by the animal till she died, unable to do much for he could not staunch the bleeding; a tennis ball wouldn't have plugged that hole. The hind died and he got to his feet feeling the bitter wind through to his bones, and as he did so a single bullet cracked above his head, then a burst ripped into the snow just short. He flung himself down as the shapeless lumps of metal hummed and whined about his ears. A man shouted somewhere close ahead and for an instant he saw the blurred flicker of a torch, then the wind came tearing up the Glen bringing fresh snow.

Far behind him the unfortunate Minister blundered about blindly in his snowed-up glassses and long black overcoat, utterly lost. Driven by the entreaties of Mrs Blair he had unwillingly left her alone and followed her husband.

"Mr Blair!" As soon make yourself heard in a steel-mill as above this wind. He was very cold and very angry. Angry that he could do nothing to help, nothing to strike a blow at the scoundrels who had ditched his car. The Reverend Sinclair let out a well-rounded and fairly un-Christian oath.

"Mr Blair!" This time the answer was the wicked howl of a ricochet. In a brief lifting of the storm he ploughed his slow way back to the road. Miserably he confessed failure to Margaret.

"It was just not possible to see nor to hear, Mrs Blair. We shall just have to wait and see what happens."

"I wish he hadn't gone off like that, on his own. Oh dear."

"Courage, Mrs Blair. Your husband will be all right. He's a man who can take care of himself." The Minister took up his position from where he could see the bridge and a short stretch of road. Beside a small roadman's hut and a great heap of stones. The wind moaned through the trees in a most melancholy fashion. He wondered briefly what his flock would think if they were to see him now, wielding a blunt instrument, crouching in a clump of trees, waiting with Mrs Blair for the coming of deer poachers. Ah, well. He sighed and pulled his tweed hat more firmly on to his head.

* * * * *

On the lower slopes of Beinn Mhor Gavin moved slowly forward, crouching with eyes screwed up against the storm, trying to see, trying to hear. But as the Minister had said, it was next to impossible. The snow-squalls were of short duration, and in the next lull he heard a man shouting and another answering from behind him. He must be in the middle of them.

"Where are you, boys?" The night cleared of a sudden and revealed the figure of a man quite close. Gavin dropped soundlessly behind a big rock and lay still. The man was carrying a rifle and stood motionless, a bulky black snowman in a greatcoat.

"Hello there," he called again. "Where are you? Shine the bloody torch, can't you?"

"Over 'ere, Johnnie." The torch winked from higher up the slope. The man shambled slowly away, stopping to prod a dead animal with his foot. Gavin left the rock and followed, keeping very low, never taking his eyes off the figure in front of him. He made a little darting run, froze as the man turned to look back. It was like grandmother's steps.

"There's one down here," the man called out. "It's——" That's as far as he got. It was the end of the game, and he had lost. Johnnie had half turned to face the sounds behind him, but too late. Gavin hurled himself at the man, landing on his back and bringing him hard to the ground. Johnnie lay still, winded and dazed by the shock of the attack. He was hauled roughly round and hit twice on the point of the jaw, exceedingly hard. Gavin dropped the limp body like a sawdust dummy, grabbed the rifle and ran to the shelter of a peat bank where he lay regaining his breath.

" 'Urry up, Johnnie boy, and give us an 'and with this lot."

From where he lay Gavin could see figures moving about on the snow some fifty yards away and slightly above him. A quarter-moon had appeared through thinning clouds and lit the scene so that up to a certain distance it could almost have been daylight. The shadows were very black. The torch flashed on and off as the poachers went about their work.

"Throw us over the axe." He heard the heavy thud of the blows as they dismembered the carcases. There was the frantic scrabble of animal legs followed by three savage blows, an 'ah, you bastard, that'll fix you', then a voice said: "Someone can't muckin' well shoot."

"Save your breath, Scrap, and get on with the job." The voice held authority, and was the one that Gavin had heard before, that first night at Hump Bridge. But somehow it struck a louder bell, though he couldn't exactly say why nor how.

"'Ow many d'you reckon we got, guv?"

"Six—seven—if we get ten away we'll have done damn well." He knew that voice, of course he knew it, but where, when?

"Christ, that's a bit of 'orl right, eh? Ten! Christ, we'll all be rolling!"

"We'll be here all night if you don't stop nattering and can't get on with it."

Someone chuckled; another one spat. The hacking up continued.

"Muckin' 'ell, this one's got an 'ide like a perishin' rhino."

"Throw us a couple o' sacks, Johnnie boy."

The cold of the snow and the night began to penetrate Gavin's town suit; his feet were ice. He wondered what to do. Alone he'd never cope with the lot of them, not even in the dark, and with this moon they'd see him as plainly as he saw them. Yet he'd got to try to keep them here. Stop them from getting back to the van. Or at least stop them getting the stuff away. He held the answer in his hands. He opened the bolt and his probing finger felt the cartridge in the breech, another lying at the top of the magazine. So far, excellent.

"That's two of them ready for carrying." The axe continued to rise and fall against the moonlit glare of the snow. Some large object was thrown into a black jumble of rocks.

"Help me up with this lot."

The man stood with a bulky load on his shoulders, bent forward like some monstrous hunchback, black and deformed. Very slowly Gavin pushed the rifle over the peat bank and drew the butt close into his shoulder. Put a rifle in his hands and Gavin Blair was happy, and supremely confident. He was a superb shot who could place a bullet pretty well exactly where he wanted; the rifle was a service type and one he knew well, added to which the sights were touched with luminous paint. Anyway, against that background a blind man couldn't miss. The foresight steadied on the hunchback. Gavin remembered his murdered rams; he remembered his wife's distress; he remembered the boat which had tried to sink them, and he was seized with a cold and savage anger. His finger tightened on the trigger. If he squeezed, the man was as dead as the pieces of meat he carried on his back. Regretfully he lowered the rifle, searching for a target. Among the rocks was one wearing a little skullcap of snow, lying a few yards to the left of the men.

Gavin aimed, between the eyes if the rock had been a face, and this time he fired. The muzzle flash was blinding and the smash of the bullet striking the rock was instantaneous with the slam of the shot. The figures stood petrified. The raised axe did not fall. They were waxwork bodysnatchers caught at their ghastly business, frozen in the strange glare of the white mountains. Then the scene burst into wild movement as the men bolted for cover. He put another bullet low above their ducking heads as they dived behind rocks and into peat-hags. He grinned to hear it whining to the stars. That ought to make them think. Not a sound. Nothing but the gentle wind across the snow and the distant thunder of the sea. Then loud whisperings. A voice called out nervously:

"Is that yourself, John Grant?"

He did not answer but swung the muzzle towards the sound.

"For God's sake, man, you'll not be needing to shoot us. We know when we're caught right enough." That would be the man Robertson.

"Whoever you are, you'd better stop this, unless you want to get hurt." There was no fear in those words. That was the leader. Gavin saw him starting to get up, then put the third bullet close as he dared to the man's head.

"Hell's teeth!" The figure disappeared rapidly. From the corner of his eye Gavin saw Johnnie slowly sit up; he groaned feebly, feeling his jaw, shaking his head. The bullet whiplashed past his ear. He fell flat, yelling with fright.

"You crummy fools," he shouted. "It's me—Johnnie!"

"Don't move, Johnnie. Lie still, for Chrissake. There's a muckin' madman out there."

Gavin suddenly screamed in a high falsetto: "If anyone moves I'll drill him, see. I'll teach you to come here and take our deer. I'll teach you. I'll kill the next man that shows his face. I'll shoot him dead, see." If they wanted a madman they could damn well have one. The scudding clouds were gathering for the next shower. In darkness he would have no chance. They would either run for it—or they would rush him. He prayed for moonlight. But his prayer was not heard, for the fringes of the fresh storm quickly covered the moon and the white glare vanished from the snow, leaving murky darkness filled with driving snowflakes. He fired one last shot to discourage them and jumped to his feet, preparing to run.

They did not rush him. Possibly because they knew they'd never find him in the whirling snow; possibly because they did not want to risk their lives. Visibility was cut to a few feet and all other sounds were swept away by that of the wind. Gavin headed back down the slope towards the road. He had to get back to the bridge before the van. His progress was hampered by the snow. Sometimes he was up to his knees. He blundered through the shallow drifts, often falling, but helped by the storm at his back, hoping to God that Margaret wouldn't do anything mad, that she'd stay hidden in the trees. He shouldn't have brought her; he shouldn't have left her like that. The snow clutched at his legs, slowing him and holding him back.

He fell again, and as he scrambled up spitting snow he heard the howl of an engine from the direction of the bridge.

* * * * *

The Reverend Andrew Sinclair was not a timid man and was simmering with righteous indignation over the ditching of his car and the painful bumping of his right knee. But when he heard the first faint sound of the engine approaching through the storm his stomach fluttered and tightened. His first thought, however. was for Margaret. He hurried to the trees.

"Mrs Blair, they are coming." She was huddling behind the inadequate shelter of a swaying tree-trunk, hugging Pusan for warmth, half-frozen by the bitter wind.

"Oh, thank goodness! I'm so cold I don't know what to do."

"You mustn't move," he entreated urgently. "I beg of you, Mrs Blair, not to move. If anything happened I—I—well, I could never face your husband again. Never." He turned his head in the direction of the road. "I must get back."

She could hear it now: the slow grinding sound of a labouring engine. Pusan began to whine and tug at his leash.

"Do be careful, Minister." The long black figure was stalking away. Oh, dear, thought Margaret, what is all this? It can't *really* be happening. Stop it, Pusan. What's happened to Gavin? Oh, dear, she thought again. Surely he's all right. He *must* be all right. The noise of the van was much closer. The Minister wiped his spectacles nervously and gripped the tyre-lever. Like Gavin he had little idea of what to do, beyond feeling he had to upset these scoundrels to the best of his ability—the rest lay in the hands of God.

The driver of the van could hardly see a foot beyond the bonnet and had considerable difficulty in keeping on the road, what with the weight of five men, the cross-wind and the snow-filled ruts. The windscreen wipers could barely cope.

"Can't you get a move on?"

"If you can drive faster, then you're welcome to the bastard."

"All right, all right," said the leader. "Keep your mind on the road and let's get out of here."

"We ain't got much out o' this trip, guv. Christ, I'd like to do the mucker what was shooting at us! Cor, 'adn't we better shift to an 'ealthier bit o' ground?" No one answered. They hung on in the bucketing van, cold and dispirited.

"Look out!"

They were on top of the car almost as they saw it blocking the bridge. With a squeal of brakes and a jolt that flung the men forward the van juddered to a skidding halt.

"Lights!"

In the headlights the car stood across the bridge: an impassable barrier.

"We'll never get past that."

"The muckin' bastard, what's 'e think 'e's playin' at?"

"Five of us. We can shove the thing out of the way."

"We'll not be needing to," interrupted Jimmy Robertson. "There's a ford. Just below the bridge it is. Go back. Go in reverse. Off the road to the right. I will tell you. I know the place well."

At that moment the Minister flung his first stone.

"If the burn is not too high——" began Robertson, then the stone hit the van. A good jagged one, thrown with considerable force, it hit the metal side with the most appalling clang. There was an outburst of startled invective from inside the vehicle; their nerves were in a bad way after the bullets.

"Muckin' 'ell, what was that?"

"I'm getting out of this."

"Stay where you are, all of you. We'll try the ford."

The van shot into reverse so fast that the next stone, aimed at the windscreen, whizzed harmlessly over the bonnet. But the Minister landed one on the roof as the van turned and made slowly off the road towards the ford.

"Easy now," implored Jimmy Robertson. "Easy does it. More left. More. Hold it. *Right!* Man alive, but we'll stick." The engine screamed, the tyres spun in the soft snow, the van gave a steep lurch to the left and they thought she was going over. Somehow the driver got her back on the hard track and down into the black water. She nosed her way into the deepening torrent that foamed round the wheels, higher and higher.

"We'll never make it, guv. She's slipping. The wheels ain't 'olding."

"We've got to make it. Keep her going, can't you?"

The Minister kept up his bombardment from the bridge. He knew he could not stop them but felt that the stones might at least serve to frighten and fluster. The dog was yelping and howling in the trees.

"Oh, well done, well done, you hit it." Margaret was beside him, dancing with excitement.

"Mrs Blair. Really you should not be——" She had gone for more stones. Pusan had slipped his collar and was in the shallows barking furiously.

"What can we do? They're getting away."

They watched the van emerge on the far side and crawl noisily back to the road beyond the bridge.

"If they stop and get out then you must run, Mrs Blair. Into the trees. They will be very angry and——" But she was not listening, she was running to meet Gavin.

"Yes, darling, I'm fine. What about you? Where's the Minister? Have they turned up? Got past? How could they? Hell, the ford." They saw the lights of the van going down the road, vanishing in the snow.

"After them," shouted the Minister. "Not a moment to be lost." Margaret ran for Chiquita while Gavin started the car. They bundled in and away, much too fast for safety. Gavin drove with his head out of the window. The Minister sat in the back urging him on. His tweed hat was pushed to the back of his head, his eyes glinted behind their spectacles.

"You were wonderful," Margaret kept saying. "You really were."

"What happened?" Gavin zigzagged madly. The Minister told him between potholes.

"It's little enough I was doing to stop them."

"Never mind," put in Margaret. "You must have hit that van about ten times." They took the corner and were over Hump Bridge, missing the parapet by inches. The road was clearer along the flats and Gavin put his foot hard down. Margaret was the first to see the van just as it disappeared round the last bend before the main road.

"Faster, Mr Blair, faster." The Minister was beside himself.

The car was gaining but very slowly. Now they could make out the van slithering badly from side to side.

"Mr Blair. Do you see? The driver has his head out. I must surely have hit the windscreen. Can we not go any faster?" He was thumping the back of the seat with clenched fists.

"Can anyone make out the number?"

"No."

"They may stop, Mr Blair. We must be ready for that."

"Not likely. Not here."

They were passing more frequent roadside cottages and crofts with lights burning behind the curtains.

"Besides, they don't know for sure it's us. We didn't catch

them up for quite a bit and we've passed two or three other cars."

"Flash your lights, darling. They might think it's a police car."

Gavin flashed them on and off, but the van driver paid no attention.

"We'll stop at the telephone box in Collalan and warn Fort Henry. They ought to get them with a patrol car."

But they never reached the village of Collalan. Just short of the main road a front tyre burst and Gavin brought the wildly careering car to a stop as the tail-light of the van vanished for the last time, well away on the Fort Henry road.

"Well, that's that. Of all the rotten bad luck!"

"If you ask me," corrected Margaret a little shakily, "what very good luck that we're still alive and in one piece."

The Minister said nothing.

"Look here," exclaimed Gavin. "Collalan's not more than about a couple of miles. I could walk it in half an hour."

"In this, Mr Blair?"

The snow was sweeping round the car and they could feel the wind whistling through the cracks and crannies.

"Of course not, Gavin. Of course you couldn't. Anyway, I shan't let you. There's only one place you're going and that's home to a hot bath and bed. Look at you, you're soaked through as it is. And there is one thing I am not going to have and that is you in hospital with pneumonia." Margaret paused, breathing heavily.

The Minister murmured agreement. "By now," he said reasonably, "they'll be in the next county. Or they will be by the time you have reached the call-box and persuaded the Collalan exchange to answer."

"But damn it all, we can't just let them drive away thumbing their noses at us."

"We did all we could, darling."

"I shouldn't have gone charging off like that. I should have stayed at the bridge, then we might have stopped them somehow." He felt utterly chilled, shivery and miserable. Hell, what was the use? He sneezed.

"Darling, get out and change that wheel and keep warm. We'll all help. It won't take long."

Gavin did not move.

"At least they didn't manage to get away with any of the deer." He sat up, suddenly more cheerful. "*And* I pinched one of their blasted rifles."

"That was indeed something, Mr Blair."

"Right, let's get this infernal wheel changed."

They got the wheel off and put on the spare. They did most of it by touch; the Minister dropped two of the nuts in the snow and by the end of it they were all thickly plastered with the driven snow. But they were warm. They steamed in the fug of the car as they drove back to the Manse. The Minister's car was deep in snow when they passed Hump Bridge.

"Murdo will come and tow it clear tomorrow. It will come to no harm. I have often left it sitting out in a winter blizzard."

The Minister's aged housekeeper met them at the door of the Manse. She was in a great taking, mumbling almost incomprehensibly between her badly fitting teeth.

"Och, gracious, you're all fair drowned. Come in, come in." She scolded the Reverend Sinclair soundly. "How was I to know what had maybe happened to you? Indeed, I was thinking the most terrible things. All the witches of Bealtuinn flying on the storm, aye, I was hearing them as I cooked the supper that's no more than a black cinder in the oven. And me thinking you were just gone out to see the Macdonalds at Famista." She followed them into the study complaining loudly.

"Calm yourself, Mrs Macleod, calm yourself. A mishap with the car, that was all. Fortunately Mr and Mrs Blair came by and rescued me from my predicament."

"Och, it's not mattering to me where you were when they

came by." She shuffled out with an aged toss of the head. Presently she shuffled back with an armful of dry clothes.

"I'll be hanging your things in the kitchen," she told Gavin. "If you come this way I'll be showing you where you can be changing."

Gavin began to protest, glancing at Margaret. "No, really. It's extremely kind but we must be going."

"You'll not be leaving this house, not in those watery horrible things." She rounded on Margaret. "Are you wanting him to die on you this very night?"

They stayed—Gavin in dry things, Margaret in a pair of the Minister's daughter's stockings. Mrs Macleod fed them on eggs and scones and pints of steaming tea. To Pusan she gave a bone and to Chiquita a bowl of warm milk. The Minister provided something a little stronger than tea. They went over the events of the evening. The Minister had to examine the rifle, aiming it at a picture of a man in a top-hat on the bookcase.

"With these sights I could be blowing my brother's hat off," he remarked facetiously.

Gavin looked across at his wife. She was curled up in a large armchair almost asleep. "I think we'd better keep everything as quiet as we can, don't you, Minister? If possible we want to keep this between ourselves and the police. Before we knew what was happening we'd have it leaking out near some newspaper chap, and the whole thing spread across the headlines, grossly exaggerated."

"And none of them would give a thought to the deer," said Margaret with her eyes shut. In the silence that followed they heard Chiquita snuffling from where she lay with her head on Pusan's shoulder.

"It is a most terrible business, Mrs Blair," said the Minister gently. "Until tonight I had no idea just how terrible."

"Come out with me tomorrow, Minister, and you'll see it even more."

"I should like to, Mr Blair, I should like to. And there are many I should like to be taking with me." He spoke very seriously. He turned the rifle over and over in his hands. "This weapon I hold here, it can be an instrument of great kindness. Or it can be an instrument of great pain and suffering and——" He did not finish, but sighed and put the rifle down abruptly.

"Another little dram, Mr Blair?"

"We've kept the Minister from his bed far too long as it is. Come along, darling, we've still got to drive home, remember?"

"I could collect my clothes when I pick you up in the morning," Gavin suggested as they went into the hall. "That is if you really want to come out with me," he added.

"I was perfectly serious, Mr Blair."

"Right. About eight then. We can catch John before he goes out."

"Don't forget the Inspector, darling, coming to lunch."

"I hadn't. What about you, Minister? Why not come back and meet the Inspector? You'd like him."

The Minister accepted.

"Oh, by the way," Margaret asked from the car, "how's Donald's 'flu?"

"He is likely to be in bed for at least another week, maybe longer, so the doctor was saying. Complications. Most unfortunate. Just at this moment, too."

"Poor Donald. He'll be terribly upset when he hears about last night."

It had stopped snowing, but the sky was heavily overcast and the clouds were rolling fast before a wind that had backed farther into the north.

"I don't like it," observed the Minister. "There's a storm on the way. A very nasty wind." He shivered and rubbed his hands. They thanked him for his hospitality.

"But it is I who should be thanking *you*, Mrs Blair. Indeed, yes. I might still be freezing in my car." He put his head close to the open window. "Rest assured, Mr Blair, I shall be more discreet than the grave itself."

He waved from his lighted doorway as they drove away. What an evening that had been, what an evening. The Reverend Sinclair went back to the warm security and peace of his Manse, hearing in his head the horrid sound of that machine-gun thing and the clang of the stones on the roof of the poachers' van.

By the time the Blairs reached home they were too tired for anything but sleep. Within half an hour they were safely in bed. Gavin set the alarm for six-thirty.

"I'll get to Bealtuinn by half-past seven," he said sleepily. "Pick up John. Then the Minister. I wonder if he does want to come—what is it, love? What's the matter? Tell me." He took his wife in his arms and tried to comfort her racking, soundless grief. She shook her head but did not answer. He stroked her hair. Then he got her a glass of water and a sleeping pill.

"Yes, Margaret, take it."

Presently she began to relax in his arms.

"It's only tiredness, darling. That's all it is. I'll be all right in the morning, really I will."

But he knew she was weeping for the agony of the wounded deer which lay out in the bloodstained snow, dying slowly and cruelly in the icy wind. And thinking of them he too came close to tears.

* * * * *

Eight badly wounded beasts staggered and limped from the shambles. One had run in mad blind circles trailing her innards through the snow till she had collapsed to die at Gavin's feet. Another, a young staggie, ran at blundering speed for a good half-mile before dropping suddenly into a deep drift where he slowly suffocated to death. Another hind hauled herself like a cut worm for a few yards with a shattered spine.

The old grey hind managed to cover perhaps a hundred

yards before her legs crumpled, pitching her forward on the hard windswept slope. Rock-flattened bullets had torn three gaping holes in her body; the lower half of her mouth had gone, carried away by a stray lump of lead, leaving a ragged stump of tongue pumping blood. She lay in the full blast of that cruel wind and the only warmth round her was her blood which melted the snow to red water.

She had roamed the mountains of Bealtuinn for thirteen years, that old hind with the grey patchy coat and the crumpled ear. She was well known to John Grant who called her Old Baldy and had conceived quite an affection for the animal which had always outsmarted him, as she did all her enemies, by the good use of her sensitive nose, the extraordinary acuteness of her ragged ears and, in the last resort, the speed of her steel-sprung legs.

Now she was finished. She would never again graze the grass in the Bay of the Splashing Seals nor walk slowly along the banks of the Black Burn as the sun came up over Creag Dhu. Never lie watchful but content with the summer sun hot on her and the flies murmuring in the heather. She would never mate with an urgent, hungry stag, nor come to drop her little spotted calf in the greeny-golden bracken.

So that men could line their pockets with silver she was maimed and suffering and finished. The curtains of snow swept over her and struck melting on her open, staring eyes. The wind howled across the frozen face of Beinn Mhor, bringing merciful death to the old animal. She died, as did the others, in great pain and great bewilderment. And the snow came to soften the harsh outlines of their stiffening carcases.

[8]

GAVIN did not get over to Bealtuinn in the morning nor did the Minister have the opportunity to see for himself the result of modern deer poaching, for his car remained in the ditch half buried in snow. Inspector Marr got no farther than the outskirts of Fort Henry on his way to Glenaila.

For just after dawn the real blizzard struck, swiftly and savagely, to block the roads and tear down every telephone line to Fort Henry and the world beyond. Gavin saw it coming as he was getting the car preparatory to fetching the stalker. He knew they were for it when he saw the trailing snow-showers in the eastern sky, wispy white beards, and the long pennant of snow-dust streaming from the summit of Beinn Bhreac, very white against the dirty leaden sky. The wind was already gusting fiercely, flattening the smoke from the chimney and rattling any doors and windows which were loose.

He looked up and, as he watched, the mountains were smothered by the blizzard. By the time he reached the gate the snow had swept down and he was cut off in a swirling confusion of raging whiteness. The house had vanished, hidden by the snow that drove horizontally in blinding curtains. The windscreen opaqued; to go on was useless. As he put the car away, he heard the muffled blare of the foghorn.

Margaret was still in bed. He did not disturb her but made himself another cup of coffee; he tried the telephone on the off-chance, but the instrument was dead and useless. Margaret came down sleepily in her dressing-gown.

"You'll never get out in this, darling."

"I know. I've tried." He sat staring gloomily out of the window.

"I'll get dressed. It looks like a day for interior decorating."

"Perhaps it'll blow itself away," he said without conviction. "These early storms sometimes do."

"I expect it will."

But it did not. For the whole of that day the blizzard tore across the Forest of Bealtuinn and for most of the next night. A blizzard unbroken by houses or trees is a truly terrifying thing, ruthless and untameable as the sea; howling across the land in blind white fury, spreading destruction and often death, and then, when it has passed, incomparable beauty. It broke over the house with a long sustained roar, plastering the walls, shutting out the daylight from the eastern windows, and sweeping away low over the invisible, raging sea.

Many of the sheep huddled in treacherous shelter, patient, enduring and stupid, doomed to die in the mounting drifts. On the bare ground of the lower slopes and in the Glen of the Skull the deer with instinctive wisdom remained in the blast of the storm and thus survived, snow-covered but unburied. But not those which lay exhausted and frozen, bleeding away what remained of their lives into the snow. That night Gavin lay for a long time worrying about his sheep and listening to the storm, trying to persuade himself that it was slackening. Twice he got up very quietly and flattened his face to the window and saw nothing in the torch beam but the rushing snowflakes.

Margaret lay awake as well. She too worried about the sheep, but she worried more about the deer she knew must be dying in that savage night while she lay snug and warm in her comfortable bed. But all she said to Gavin was: "Try and sleep, darling. There's nothing you can do."

He got back beside her. She put his hand to her breast and whispered soothing words, and at length he fell into an uneasy sleep broken by the final fury of the blizzard before it began to die away.

By morning the wind had dropped and the snow had

stopped falling, leaving a scene of quite spectacular beauty. The road was impassable and the approaches to the hills piled high with drifted snow. Gavin did what he could to clear round the house, much impeded by Chiquita. She was fascinated by this strange white stuff which stuck to her face and got up her nose and suddenly clutched her round the legs. He opened a pathway to the henhouse and the coalhole; he fed hay to his cattle and threw scraps to the hungry gulls.

The sky was clear and cold and there was a thin crust to the snow; icicles hung from the gutters and the water in the cattle trough was frozen. Later in the morning he and Margaret walked over to Bealtuinn by the shore path. Chiquita followed for a short way, then panicked, shook her head so that the little bell rang shrilly, and trotted back to the safety of the byre.

"Yes, love, of course she'll be all right. No one can get here by land and certainly not by sea. Stop fussing, woman." The sea was big, chunky and steep, not the usual slow Atlantic sweep. "No boat could live in that."

They walked fast to keep warm, with Pusan delirious with excitement ranging up and down the hard sands. Beinn Bhreac was hidden by cloud wrack, just the very summit. They searched the lower slopes with glasses but saw no sheep.

"Let's hope they had the sense to get into the Chasm during the worst of it. Or below the lee of Beinn Mhor. Otherwise I'm afraid we'll have lost a good few. As soon as the snow gets easier I'll be tramping the hills for days as far as I can see. Hell, I wish we'd got them down before this happened. I'm a fat lot of use as a shepherd!"

"You couldn't have known, darling."

"You've got to know these things. Like we should know about these poachers, instead of being caught with our pants down each time. It's all come at once: that business the other night and now this damned snow mucking everything up. We're so infernally cut off on these occasions. Not even a telephone. I'll have to get to Fort Henry somehow and see Marr. Donald's a broken reed, stuck there in his bed. I want to take John out to Beinn Mhor, and the Minister. D'you think he meant it?"

"Yes, I do."

"There's Mike too, he'll have to be told. It's all going to take too long, when I ought to be concentrating on the sheep. Here, hey, Pusan! Come out of that!"

They were skirting the Quaking Sands. White ice showed among the rushes giving the place a certain sinister beauty. The ruined cottage was softened by the snow, and the hillock where they had eaten their picnic was a white beehive. Pusan nosed among the frosted crackling seaweed. All the little hollows were filled with wreaths of snow, and deep white bridges spanned the burns so that the water rushed through frozen blue-green tunnels. The harshness of the land was buried and hidden beneath the snow, over which there lay a hard glittering sheen. Their footsteps broke through, leaving shallow prints edged with jagged crumbly ice, tinged with that strange bluey-greenness.

They looked up the long white valley of Skull Glen.

"It is lovely, isn't it, darling?"

"Mmm." His answer was preoccupied.

She linked her arm in his. "I know it's all terribly worrying," she said, "but perhaps John'll have some ideas."

The stalker was in his shirt sleeves, slowly clearing his path. As he saw them approaching he stopped and got out his little black pipe, laying aside his shovel in pleasant Highland anticipation of a smoke and a gossip.

"Aye, a lot of snow was falling right enough. But it'll not be lying for very long I'm thinking. Not at this time of the year. It's yourself that's looking well, Mrs Blair." He looked down at the small figure in its sheepskin jacket, trousers and child-size rubber boots. As a rule he was not approving of trousers for women. They were giving them the wrong ideas altogether, but Mrs Blair now . . . He smiled at her. He did not smile, however, when Gavin had finished telling him about the poachers.

"Man alive, so they've been back. And me knowing not a thing about it." He shook his head ruefully. "I was not hearing a thing either. But Mrs Grant she was telling me that she had heard a shot, and there was I saying she was after dreaming it. Och, if I could only have been there, Mr Blair. Shooting at them, you say? And you have the little devil's rifle. Man, but that was very good work. Was it not good work, Mrs Blair?"

"Yes, very."

"Aye, it was that. Shooting at them," he repeated wistfully. "If they had been Jerries now you could have been aiming at them." He drew thoughtfully on his pipe. "So that's the second time these fellows have been running and leaving dead deer behind. They'll not be liking that, Mr Blair, not at all. These are not men who will be wanting to leave Bealtuinn without something for their trouble. Indeed, we'll need to be watching out with all our eyes. Aye, I'm thinking we'll be hearing more from the wicked little fellows before the winter's through."

"We've got to stop them," said Gavin. "That's twice they've got away with killing deer. God knows how many they hit this time."

"We'll be going out to Beinn Mhor first thing we can, Mr Blair." He squinted up at the cold sky. "This will have been killing the wounded beasts fairly quickly. But there may be some that have not died."

"Don't," protested Margaret.

"I am sorry, Mrs Blair. I am knowing well how you feel. It is how we all feel." He clenched his huge hands. "Och, if I could only be getting close to these devils. If you and me and Kenny Carmichael there and Captain Downie, if we just could be catching them one night, man, I'm telling you we would not be needing any bloody policeman or silly wee sheriff to do the job for us."

"Obviously the person to watch is that Robertson creature," said Margaret. "I mean, we know he was with them."

"Do we?"

"Of course we do, Gavin. We saw him getting into the van."

"Yes, I know, but we didn't see him getting out."

"Getting out?"

"He may only have been having a lift home for all we know."

"No, I'm thinking Jimmy's mixed up with them right enough. It is just the sort of business he would be joining. But he will be knowing that I know and that many other people hereabouts are having their suspicions. No, he will not be doing anything to draw attention to himself, not for a wee while at least. We could maybe let Donald into the secret and be watching ourselves to see if the fellow is taking the bus to Fort Henry, or if any strangers are to be seen at his croft."

"We could follow him and see who he meets."

"Aye, Mrs Blair, you are the born detective right enough."

They laughed.

"Right then. As soon as we can get there we'll go along to Beinn Mhor——"

"And *I'll* go into Fort Henry and see the Inspector," interrupted Margaret firmly. "If necessary, I'll bring him out with me."

"Och, I am telling you, Mr Blair, she will soon be wearing one of them little policemen's hats."

So they left it at that: all future plans depending on the going or the staying of the snow.

They did not have long to wait. By the evening of that same day the thaw was brought in the skirts of a warm west wind. All through the night the brittle beauty turned to slush, and where the snow had not lain deep the bare wet ground showed in dark patches. Water ran in the gutters of the house, the icicles shortened and finally vanished and the snow fell—*plumph*—from the roof in great inert lumps. The burns torrented down from the mountains, grey and soapy and swollen; melting snow rushed in fresh floods down every steep slope and the whole land was loud with the sound of tumbling water. By the morning a steady drizzle was falling from a lowering sky. But in the hollows and in the lee of great rocks and high banks the snow was still piled deep, and below the slowly melting surface lay dead sheep.

On every vantage point in the Forest there perched a raven or a grey crow or a buzzard alert for what the dwindling of the snow might reveal.

* * * * *

The cloud of black scavengers rose flapping and croaking from the feast as the three men made their way from the road up the lower slope of Beinn Mhor. The going was not easy, for a good deal of slushy snow remained into which they often slipped. It was the Minister who came upon the first sign of butchery. He stood looking at the severed head without speaking before he called the others. Gavin cleared away the snow and came upon another, the head of a calf, shot through the back of the neck. In all they found eight heads. It was as though some monstrous great guillotine had been at work; a guillotine with a blunt and jagged blade. The Minister was shocked by what he saw, and said so. John Grant smiled grimly to himself. Man alive, he thought, if you're never seeing anything worse than this in your life you'll not need to be grumbling. The Minister had seen worse; much worse. He had been in London during the worst of the *blitz*. But he was still very shocked.

"It's terrible," he kept repeating, shaking his head as though in disbelief, "really terrible. Why, it's like a—a battlefield."

The melting snow covered a shambles. Here and there lengths of intestines lay coiled like grey cord, pulled into view by the feasting birds. Gavin found three large sacks: one empty, the others each containing two blackening haunches.

The watery sun came out. The splash and drip of water sounded all round them and the ravens circled, complaining raucously at being robbed of their meal. The Minister sat down on a rock; he pushed the tweed hat to the back of his head and unbuttoned his coat.

"Well," remarked the stalker, coming to join him, "that is nine they were killing."

"Ten," said Gavin. "There's one lying near the road."

"Ten." John Grant got out his little black pipe. His thick eyebrows were drawn together by his anger, and the downward crescent of his mouth was very pronounced in the depths of his beard. He spat into the snow.

"Ten," he repeated for the third time. "Man, but it is enough to make a man sick in the stomach." He lit the pipe; then he got out his old glass and began to spy across the Flats. The Minister traced patterns in the slushy snow with the tip of his walking-stick.

"Well, Minister," said Gavin quietly, "now you've seen what deer poaching really means. Not exactly John Macnab stuff, is it?" He threw a stone at a hoodie perched on a rock.

"Surely they will not get away with this?" The Minister gestured at the ugly remains.

"Not if we are having anything to do with it," growled the stalker, snapping shut his glass.

"There are a lot of people I should like to bring here," the Minister said vehemently.

"The ones that should be dragged here by the backs of their bloody wee necks are the sheriffs who let these damned murdering fellows out of their courts with a warning and a—och, I'd be rubbing their sharp noses in it right enough." He banged the pipe furiously against his boot. "Sitting up there, so grand and important in their high chairs, talking so loud and doing not a thing at all, being paid for dishing out a lot of nonsense.

What do they know about the deer, they and their silly daft laws? Damned little, I'm telling you, Minister, damned little."

"Oh, come now, John, some of them are good men. They are not all as you describe," protested the Minister mildly.

"Maybe not. But why are they not handing out some proper punishment then? Answer me that, Minister. Och, I'm telling you, it's yourself that should be doing something."

"I, John? What should I do?"

"Speak out about this from the pulpit," said Gavin calmly. "Stir people's consciences—if they've still got such things in this great day and age. Get them interested. Get them angry. Anything, but get them to listen. After all, Minister, you've got an audience."

"What you are advocating in fact is that I should use the pulpit for the stirring up of passions and——"

"It has been used to stir up worse ones," Gavin interrupted hotly. "Surely if the Church can't speak out against cruelty it might just as well—it might just as well pack up."

The Minister glanced at the other's taut, angry face. The stalker slowly refilled his pipe, looking out towards Creag Dhu, saying nothing, wondering how the Minister would answer that. The latter watched the antics of half a dozen ravens playing in the sky, wheeling and swooping.

"You think I should go into my pulpit and preach a crusade against these men?" he asked gently.

"Not just these ones." Gavin plucked a stem of dead grass and began to chew. Suddenly he laughed. "You think I'm round the bend, don't you?"

"No, Mr Blair, I do not think you're—er—round the bend, as you put it. You feel this very deeply, don't you?"

"Very, yes."

"Both you and Mrs Blair feel that the whole community's to blame by its lack of interest, its smug complacency shall we say, its shrugging of the shoulders and nothing-to-do-with-us attitude."

"Exactly."

"But, you, I think, are prepared to do more about it than just shout angrily. That I saw the other night."

"So are you, Minister. Or you wouldn't have pelted that van with stones. Remember?"

"Man, but what are you saying?" The stalker regarded the Minister with astonishment tinged with admiration.

"Well, well. So you were throwing stones at them." The pipe gurgled and spluttered.

"I should be grateful, John, if you would keep that piece of information to yourself."

"Aye, Minister, I'll not be telling another soul. Throwing stones. Well, well." The stalker's eyes twinkled.

"I shall think about what you were saying," said the Minister after a pause. "What I have seen here today has given me much to ponder. Indeed, it has opened my eyes a good deal wider." A breath of colder wind made him fasten his coat and pull down his tweed hat firmly on his head. "Will Mrs Blair have seen that inspector fellow yet, are you thinking, Mr Blair?"

Gavin consulted his watch. "She should be with him now."

"I imagine that he will come out to see for himself," said the Minister.

"Probably. By the way, I looked in and saw Donald this morning. He's pretty groggy still and won't be on the road for at least another week. I told him everything except about you, Minister. I don't suppose you want to get too much involved?"

"No, Mr Blair. Let us, shall we say, keep it in the family."

Gavin jumped to his feet. "I've got to go and have a look for my sheep. They're in pretty good chaos after the storm. I'll keep you posted, John."

"Aye, Mr Blair, and I will do the same." He took a quick look at the sky. "I'm thinking the deer will be going back to the tops. With this wind the snow will not be lying long."

"You going straight to Bealtuinn now?"

The stalker shook his head. "Not until I have had a look for wounded beasts. If you should be seeing the Captain, would you be telling him from me that the hen food he was ordering from Fort Henry has come to Bealtuinn? It is that new driver, he's never knowing whether it is Monday or Friday at all."

"The Captain's in the infirmary in Inverness."

"Really?" said the Minister. "I am very sorry to hear that. Nothing serious, I hope?"

"Trouble with a wisdom tooth. He ought to be home in a day or two."

"Well, we are going down like the proverbial ninepins," said the Minister. "What with Donald and now Captain Downie. Let us hope they will be back on their feet soon in case"—he tapped a severed hoof with his stick—"in case this should happen again. If it does, we shall need all our forces."

"That's the spirit I'm liking, Minister." The stalker's smile was approving.

"Thank you, John. Now I must return to my more routine duties. But rest assured that I shall certainly keep my eyes and ears open. Should anything at all suspicious come to my notice, then I'll let you both know at once."

They watched him to his car.

"A good man, the Minister," conceded the stalker. "A very good man indeed."

"He is."

They went as far as the big rowan tree together, then the stalker made for Creag Dhu and Gavin, whistling to his dog, headed down the Glen of the Skull.

He climbed along the western face of Sgurr Bheag above the Wailing Loch and came upon some thirty sheep high up. Pusan drove them down on to the flat ground. The drifts in the hollows were still deep enough to hide any number of sheep; it would only be when the ground was bare that he would see what losses he had suffered in the blizzard. Sufficient unto the day. There was nothing he could do. Gavin descended to the shores of the Wailing Loch. The water was blacker than ever against the snow-patches; the place was quite deserted and very cold out of the sun.

But it was not deserted. A stag lurched to its feet some way in front of him and stumbled away on three legs. Gavin signalled to Pusan. The dog streaked for the hillside, to get above the animal. Gavin loaded a round into the breech of his rifle and followed very slowly. He could see the stag would not go far; he could also see the switch horns, twin curves of bone without branching points, deadly as rapiers.

The beast was very weak from loss of blood, hunger and exposure. It thrashed its desperate way through a stretch of snow, leaving a scarlet trail from the reopened wound in its shoulder. Pusan uttered a short bark and the stag raised its gaunt head at the sound, but it did not see so well any more, for the soft brown eyes were blurred by weakness, its senses dulled by the tearing pain of the festered wound. It stopped and stared helplessly into the swimming foreground.

The collie came at the stag in a fierce, fast rush. The cripple turned to meet the attack it could hardly see, lowering the lethal horns and thrusting upwards with the last of its strength. Pusan saved himself from impalement by a frantic twist in the air as he leapt for the throat. He fell on his side, but was up in a flash, snarling with bared teeth and savage yellow eyes. The stag's life was pouring in a rich dark flood from the wound and all it could do was to jerk feebly at its enemy.

Pusan edged closer, body hugging the ground, ears flat, the snarl rumbling in his throat. Back went the stag, foot by foot, clumsy on three legs, back, back till it felt the icy water round its hind feet. Twice the dog sprang with a vicious snap of teeth; twice he twisted himself clear of those skewer horns. The hindquarters of the stag dropped lower into the waters of the Wailing Loch. Now it could no longer move, for the grip of the muddy sand was tightening round the weak and trembling legs. The wretched beast snorted pathetic defiance at the dog and at the man standing close beyond. The man suddenly shouted and the stag raised its head for the last time to meet the merciful bullet at the base of the horns. It dropped, rolling sideways beneath the surface; for a moment the body threshed the water to red foam, then it slid out of sight leaving only the horns sticking like two black reeds from the surface.

Gavin tried to drag the stag ashore, with Pusan splashing and barking in the shallows, but he could not manage it. Wind stroked the silent loch and at once the air was filled with the unearthly sound that gave the place its name. Pusan whimpered and crept closer to his master.

"It's all right, I don't like it either." Dark clouds covered the sun; the wind blew harder and the sound grew louder and more strident. A sombre red stain was flowering on the black water. Gavin shivered and patted his trembling dog. Two ravens swooped from the darkening sky into the bleached skeleton tree on the island. One of them croaked harshly and flew to the shore to be nearer death, nodding its head in anticipation.

Gavin went on his way thinking bitterly of the terrified, hopeless look in the stag's eyes. Above him a long line of deer, disturbed by the shot, were plunging across the white face of the Little Sister, belly-deep in the snow. He followed round the top of the loch between the Sisters, and so home.

* * * * *

Margaret was not back from Fort Henry. For a moment he was worried, then he remembered she might be going on to visit Mike in the infirmary. After a quick bread-and-cheese meal he went out again and spent till evening checking on his sheep. The greatest number, over two hundred, were concentrated at the foot of Beinn Bhreac, between the mountain and the sea. Provided they remained there they would come to no harm. One ewe he spotted higher up stuck on a ledge above a steep rock-face. By the time he had got her to safety the sun was well down behind the islands.

The car stood at the door. Margaret was in the kitchen preparing supper.

"Darling, you look dead. Come and sit quietly with a drink and tell me about the sheep."

They relaxed by the fire. Pusan stretched out on the rug; Chiquita curled up in her basket.

"And how was your day?" Gavin asked.

"Moderately successful. Our Inspector was out, but I saw a very large sergeant——"

"That must have been Georgison. He's Donald's brother-in-law. Well, anyway, what did you tell him?"

"I said we'd had the poachers back and that some more deer had been killed and that we'd chased the van but it had got away on the Fort Henry road. That's all."

"Nothing about the rifle?"

"No."

"You didn't mention the Minister?"

"No."

"Just as well. What did the law say?"

"Oh, that he'd make out a report for the Inspector and that we'd probably be hearing more in the near future. I told him our telephone lines were like mixed-up knitting wool. Actually they're mending it between Rappoch and the main road."

"Good lord, someone's had a new lease of life. It's usually about ten days before anyone even notices they're down. I expect Marr'll probably come out tomorrow."

"Oh, yes, darling, before I forget, Mike asked if one of us could pick him up tomorrow."

"How was he?"

"A bit swollen still and talking rather funnily. He was tossing about all over the place like a bull that's been kept in a pen too long, bellowing out of a pumpkin face."

"Did you tell him about Thursday night?"

"Not much, no. He's in a ward full of the most extraordinary old men you've ever seen, all lying there pretending to be asleep and listening to every word. I said we'd had a bit of excitement and left it at that."

"Tell you what," said Gavin, "I'll pick him up and we'll call in and see Marr on the way home."

The Inspector was in his office next day and was delighted to see them. Introductions and small talk over, they got down to business. Marr listened quietly as Gavin talked, now and then making a note on a small pad. Most of the time he tapped his teeth gently with the pencil and stared at the ceiling.

"That's all, I think," concluded Gavin.

"Hmm," murmured the Inspector, glancing at the pad, then back at the ceiling. Gavin had not mentioned the fact he had used the rifle which lay across the end of the table. Marr pointed at it suddenly.

"I wonder how many of those damned things are sculling about unlicensed."

"Plenty," said Mike. "The place is stiff with them. Always has been."

Marr sat forward with his elbows on the table.

"Very well, then, the position as I see it is this." He opened a drawer and drew out a folder and sat for a moment studying the contents. He picked up a paper knife and, holding it like a dagger, softly stabbed the point into his blotter to emphasise the various points. "Number of incidents, four. Net results from poachers' point of view, pretty feeble. They've killed a certain number of deer and have had to leave practically the whole lot behind. They have—as far as we know—killed two of your rams. They have, it appears, tried either to frighten you or to drown you, probably the former. On at least two occasions one of these men has fired at you." He addressed his remarks to Gavin.

"They know the country. Or, rather, they have employed a man who does. Incidentally we have discovered one thing about this man Robertson: he spends a very great deal of money on drink. Men who drink to excess are inclined to talk to excess. We might get some sort of a lead from there."

"He was sacked from Famista for drinking and spreading stories about old Colonel Mackenzie," volunteered Mike. The Inspector did not answer.

"God's sakes," he exclaimed loudly, stabbing with his paper knife. "You wouldn't think it possible, would you? They drive in, blaze away and drive out again, and all in a place where every Tom, Dick and Harry knows if every other T, D and H so much as blow their bloody noses."

"Of course," suggested Gavin, "none of the deer have been sold yet, so we've got nothing to go on that end either."

"There's nothing to go on at any bloody end."

"Can't quite understand," said Mike, "why these jokers cut up the deer the other night. Surely no dealer's going to take bits and pieces."

"Hmm," said Marr. "I don't know. They can carry more meat in the van without the heads and legs."

"This idea of a hideout somewhere, a farm perhaps, d'you think there's anything in it, Inspector?" Mike asked.

"Could be. If there is, then it must be a long way from here?"

"Why?"

"We'd have heard something by now."

A constable brought in tea and biscuits. Marr walked about the room drinking his tea.

"It's a sod," he remarked. "A real sod. There's a hell of a lot to go on, yet there's absolutely damn all. The only hope's to get a tip-off and catch 'em on the job."

"But I have caught them on the job," Gavin pointed out. "Twice."

"*We've* got to catch 'em," answered the Inspector brusquely. He bit savagely at a biscuit, scattering a shower of crumbs over his tunic. "We traced the boat by the way," he went on. "In Lochinver. Black, with a bright yellow wheel-house."

"That's her."

"A few discreet inquiries, nothing official, merely discovered the fact that the boat had been in port on the day and date in question. Naturally. Net mending or painting. No, the skipper said, no, he was never taking his boat to that part of the coast at all. It was too dangerous altogether."

"Another dead end," said Gavin.

The Inspector nodded. "Look here," he suggested. "Can you watch this chap Robertson from your end? It's no use Constable McPhail doing it. If he thinks he's under observation he won't make a move."

"He may get desperate."

"Desperate?"

"Money," Gavin explained. "For drink."

"Possible."

"They'll lie doggo for a bit after this last carry-on." Mike chewed cautiously with his swollen jaw. "I'd lay a fiver his pals have told him to keep away for the time being. I reckon they'll give it a week or two for the dust to settle."

"I think you're right, Captain. Personally I'm not sure they won't clear out to pastures new and a good deal quieter. Damn it all, this isn't the only deer forest in the country."

"No," objected Gavin. "But it's the only one so full of deer. The place is crawling with them at the moment. Besides, these don't strike me as being the sort of men to give up just because someone gets in their way. They're much more likely to be working out some new plan."

"Hmm." The Inspector looked out of the window, watching the inhabitants of Fort Henry go by. He watched a man walk slowly along the opposite pavement, a man with very thick blond hair who stopped often to gaze idly into shop-windows with his pale blue eyes.

"Well," he said, "it looks as if we'll just have to wait and see. They must have money coming from somewhere. They can't live on air and a few dead deer they haven't been able to sell. God's sakes"—he struck his fist against his open hand —"you'd think it would be simple enough to——" The telephone shrilled.

"Inspector Marr. Yes, who's speaking, please?" The others saw his expression change as he listened. He began to write on the pad.

"Yes . . . where did you say? Yes, I've got that. No, but I'll find it on the map. Yes . . . yes . . . what was that last bit? Would you speak up, please?" He shook the receiver impatiently. "That's better. Yes . . . yes. I see. Thank you. Would you give me your name, please?" Gavin heard a click at the other end. "Hello . . . hello . . . damn!" Marr called the exchange. "Try and trace that call, please." He leant back in his chair.

"Well," he said slowly. "Talk of the devil. You may be interested to know that a van, dark blue or black, number illegible, was seen last night parked by the side of the road near some place called——" he consulted his pad, and spelt out the word: "D-U-A-L-A-I-N-N. Dualainn."

"Hang on," said Mike. "I know that name. It's over beyond Kylestrome. Must be about twenty miles from here. What was the van doing?"

"Four men were seen loading carcases into it."

"Were any shots heard?"

"He didn't say."

"They certainly get about," Mike said. "Dualainn's on Invershin. Doesn't even march with Bealtuinn."

"May not be the same chaps," said Gavin.

"Sounds like 'em all right. Van and all. Looks as if they may have shifted ground." The telephone rang again.

"Not much help," said Marr, putting down the receiver. "Public call box. Anonymous assistance from a public benefactor. For all we know he may have been making it up. They often do."

"Or someone doing it on purpose," put in Gavin.

They left the Inspector, promising to keep their eyes open, and drove to Famista without feeling that they had achieved much. On the outskirts of the town they were passed by a large shooting-brake going the same way. Gavin recognised the blond hair of the driver.

"That's the chap we met the other day in the Station Hotel."

Mike grunted. His face was hurting and he wanted to get home. "Seems in a hell of a hurry."

"I wonder who he is?" The brake vanished round the next corner, sending up sprays of brown water from the puddles.

Mike grunted again. "Come up for the fishing, old boy." He hugged his swollen jaw. "Rich type." He relapsed into silence for the rest of the way.

The blond man was a rich type, but he was not up for the fishing.

[9]

For the next week or so, well into November, the weather remained open but very cold with the threat of snow that piled heavily in the eastern sky but never came. There was little sun, and daylight faded very early into dark grey dusks. The deer were gathered in the corries, feeding on the Flats, in the Sanctuary and along the river, not venturing too high. For snow still clung stubbornly to the tops and along the northern faces of the mountains.

Life went forward as it always has in the West Highlands, the life which has gone forward for centuries at the same slow, dreamy pace, unperturbed by storm, war or pestilence. It seemed as though Inspector Marr had been right and that the poachers had in fact shifted their attentions elsewhere. He received no more telephone calls, and though many inquiries were set in train, both official and otherwise, nothing concrete came of them. Besides, Marr himself was engaged in a particularly nasty case of robbery with violence and had little time to spare for deer poaching.

One day Sergeant Georgison paid a call upon the man Aeneas Macdonald, that red-faced old rogue of a butcher and dealer in game.

"So it's yourself, Sergeant Georgison. It's very glad I am to see you. You'll be joining me in a wee sensation?" They went through into the back room where Aeneas kept a supply of wee sensations with which to cement bargains and oil throats and the like. The sergeant seated himself before the fire and removed his cap. The sensations were poured, then, the first smacking of lips and sighs of contentment got over, they discussed the weather, mutual acquaintances, the shockingly low price of beef and Aeneas's arthritic joints; they inquired respectfully after each other's wives and children. Then there was a short silence, during which the butcher watched the policeman from the corners of his shrewd little eyes and wondered what he was after.

"You'll not have been having much venison this year," remarked the sergeant. "Donald McPhail was telling me John Grant was saying there have been very few stags killed this season."

"And how is himself? Donald? I was hearing he has been down with the influenza. A very nasty thing indeed."

"He is better now."

"Indeed I am glad. Aye, a very unpleasant disease."

They considered the fact for a little while.

"It is true right enough," growled the old man in his hoarse, throaty voice, "I have not had my hands on more than half a dozen good stags since the end of September."

"Well now, that is a pity."

"Aye. It is time they English fellows were coming back to Bealtuinn. They were always after taking the fattest beasts on the Forest."

"And them taking no more than the horns to stick in their bloody great houses down south. Is that not right?"

"Aye."

They considered that.

"But," said Georgison, squinting through his empty glass, "there are always the poaching lads."

Aeneas chuckled. "Now, Sergeant, what would I be knowing about such things?"

"Are they not selling the stuff to you any more then?" Georgison chuckled. "Is it too big a price they are asking of you, Mr Macdonald?"

The old man quivered like an indignant red jelly. "Now what sort of a remark is that?" he puffed, blinking his sharp little eyes.

"We'll have been knowing each other a long time, Mr

Macdonald. There is no need to be getting angry now. It is well known that poached venison is just as good to eat or to put in tins as the other kind. And I'm thinking the money's just the same rich colour."

"I'm telling you, Sergeant, I've had no more than half a dozen stags this season. And all of them coming from Invershin. You can be asking Dugald Macintyre himself."

"No hinds, Mr Macdonald? No poor wee calfies?"

"They know better than to be bringing me hinds before December," protested the butcher piously.

"You would be coming straight to us. Is that not a fact, Mr Macdonald?"

"I'm thinking your memory is failing, Sergeant. Do you not remember the last time when——"

"Aye," interrupted Georgison, "I am remembering well enough. And if you were seeing strangers, Mr Macdonald, who were after bringing you deer, you would not be forgetting to let us know now, would you?"

The fat old man raised his little eyes to the ceiling, asking Heaven to forgive the gross insinuations of this uniformed barbarian. "If there has been poaching hereabouts they have not been bringing the deer to me." He poured another, slightly bigger sensation.

There, like everywhere else, Sergeant Georgison came up against a blank wall.

Over in Bealtuinn, John Grant spent the dawns and the dusks in watching. He watched the sea, he watched the roads—and he watched Jimmy Robertson. But he saw nothing suspicious; not a thing. The sea was grey and the swell heavy, and the only boats kept well clear of the coast. The roads were empty save for the local traffic. And as for Robertson, he worked slowly at his road-mending and poured his wages down his throat as he had been doing since he returned from Stornoway.

"You'll be finding this a wee bit of a change, Jimmy," said Grant one day, from his car.

The other leant on his shovel.

"I'll not be saying I enjoy it." The man had a breath on him like a leaky still, thought Grant. They spoke in Gaelic. "But it is a living. And I can be watching the deer," he added bitterly. "Man, but there are times that I miss them." He sounded as if he meant it.

"You'll have to be keeping your eyes open for these poaching rascals." And him hardly able to see out of his eyes for the pools of whisky in them. Robertson muttered something and went back to his slow shovelling of stones.

The stalker came upon the remains of another two animals. One had fallen into a deep cleft in the rocks and must have starved to death there; the other's bones had been picked almost clean.

But no strangers were seen; no boats skulked in the bays and inlets of the Bealtuinn shore; no shots split the darkness. As winter closed down upon the land, the deer were left in peace. Mike Downie's swollen face subsided to its normal shape. He, like Gavin, was busy preparing for winter. The latter tramped many miles trying to keep his sheep from the lure of the high ground where death lay in wait should another blizzard strike. In the first one he had lost at least fifteen ewes.

The Minister spoke out fiercely from his pulpit, taking as his theme man's inhumanity to the lower creatures. But, as he remarked to Gavin afterwards, he rather doubted if his words had taken much effect upon the twenty-three impassive members of his congregation.

"Maybe it will persuade them to be a little more kindly to their hens for a few days," he said with a smile.

"No one said anything about it afterwards?"

"Duncan McAlister hobbled up and said, 'That was a strong sermon you were giving us, Minister.' Then he said, 'But you'll surely not be expecting us to be running over the hills after these fellows ourselves.' " He smiled again and asked:

"There have been no new developments?"

"Not a thing."

"They are saying there has been poaching across on Invershin."

"So I believe, yes."

"Let us hope they have decided to leave us in peace, Mr Blair."

"Perhaps the Minister over there isn't so accurate with his stones." They both laughed.

The next day Constable McPhail ventured out for the first time since he had left his bed of sickness, and his first port of call was the shop where he found Kenny and Gavin arguing about the relative merits of various galvanised buckets.

"And how's yourself, Donald?" Kenny beamed.

"Och well, better, thank you, Kenny. But my legs are made of cotton-wool. There is no strength in them at all." He sat himself down on the chair provided for the aged and infirm. The policeman was dressed informally in tweed jacket and uniform trousers.

"Nice to see you up again," said Gavin.

"Aye, and it's nice to be seeing the sun again after lying helpless like a sheep on its back for this long while."

They heard steps outside and the shop bell rang.

"Well, well, and how are things with you on this topper of a day, Jimmy?"

James Robertson stood uncertainly in the doorway, looking from one to the other. Then he slowly shambled forward. He was more down-at-heel and decrepit than usual, with a gingery stubble thick on his grey face and the traces of last night's drinking still swimming in his small red eyes. He put his hands on the counter and stared glassily at the goods, belching every now and then without much enthusiasm.

"You're not looking well at all," observed Kenny, with a wink at Donald.

"I'm well enough." The man swayed slightly. Sweat stood out on his face, sickly as dirty glycerine. "An ounce of the black twist," he said thickly. At the thought of such a thing his skin turned to olive.

"Man, but the sweat's pouring from you like beer from a leaky barrel. You'd best be seeing the doctor, Jimmy."

Robertson grunted.

"If you smoke this today," chuckled Kenny, pushing across the little packet, "it's the Minister you'll be needing. Isn't that right, Mr Blair?"

Gavin smiled. Robertson glared but did not speak.

"That'll be four and twopence," said Kenny.

The man swore.

"You should be sticking to lemonade," advised Donald, "and saving your pocket—and your head. It'll have been a heavy night I'm thinking."

Another grunt.

"Four and twopence," repeated Kenny.

Robertson let out a pretty foul oath and fumbled in his pocket. "That's a bloody wicked price for a few wee pipefuls," he grumbled.

"But you'll not be missing it, eh, Jimmy boy? Not with the great wages they're after paying you on the roads. For growing corns on your chest, leaning on the shovel all day."

The other slapped down a pound note. "I'll ask you for the change and you can be keeping your bloody jokes to yourself, Kenny Carmichael."

Kenny's eyes hardened to ice-chips; but he folded his arms across his broad chest and answered levelly enough. "They're telling me there's always extra money to be made these days. If you know where to go, eh, Mr Blair?"

"Very likely."

Donald tapped his fingers slowly on the counter, watching Robertson through half-closed eyes.

"There's money to be made from the deer now. Or so I'm hearing." Kenny leant forward across the counter. "You're a man knowing about such things. There's very few men are knowing the deer better than yourself. Now, Jimmy, what are you thinking? These poacher fellows that have been to Bealtuinn, will they be coming back are you thinking?"

Robertson's eyes fell before the hard blue stare, then darted a sideways glance at Donald, but the policeman was interesting himself in a tray of home-made fudge.

"No," he muttered. "No, they'll not be back." He belched disgustingly and wiped his face with a dirty rag of a handkerchief.

"And what makes you so sure, Jimmy? The deer are thick as bees on honey this year. They'll always be finding beasts to shoot. So why should they not be coming back?"

"You want to know? All right then, I'll be telling you. After the New Year. In the hard weather, that's when they'll be back. And good luck to them," he suddenly shouted defiantly. "Bloody good luck to them, I say. They're men needing the money like the rest of us." He grimaced, showing his long yellow fangs in what was meant for a smile. "Just you be listening to me, Kenny Carmichael. When I was your age I was the best stalker between here and Inverness. There was not another man who knew the deer as I did then. I was knowing the stags on Famista like a mother's knowing her own children. I was looking after them all the months of the year, aye, I was. And what was I getting for all my devotion but the bloody sack. That's what I got—the bloody sack. Christ, he's a drunken old bastard, Jimmy Robertson, but he used to love his bloody deer. But now—now I'm not caring a bloody damn for them!" He blew his nose loudly.

"Och," said Kenny kindly, "you're not needing to take it so hard, Jimmy."

But Robertson did not listen; he turned to Donald. "You'll need to be after them, Constable McPhail. Watching all night you'll be, freezing your bloody great boots in the snow. And you might as well be keeping to your bed, I'm thinking, as chasing after these lads. You'll be needing an aeroplane to be catching them, I'm telling you, Donald McPhail."

He started for the door, stopped, swayed and placed a grimy finger along his nose. "He's too damned drunk to find his way home—that's what you're thinking, isn't it? Aye, I can see it in all your bloody faces. But just you listen to me, who knows every inch of the country as you're knowing the shape of your own bloody backsides, while I tell you——" He broke off, swallowing hard.

"And what is it you'll be after telling us, Jimmy?" asked Donald encouragingly.

"I'm telling you—I'm telling you when the snow is deep in the Glen of the Skull, right down to the sea, then——" He lurched quickly out of the door, swallowing harder.

Kenny's mouth curled in disgust. "Well, well, the wee fellow's very full of talk today, and him with a head on him like a concrete mixer."

"A bit too talkative, if you ask me," said Gavin.

Kenny looked puzzled.

"He seemed a bit too keen to share his ideas."

"He was still that drunk he was making no sense at all."

"I don't know, Donald. I may be wrong, but I don't think he was half as bad as he made out. All that stuff about after the New Year——" A car drew up outside.

John Grant came through the door.

"So you're back again, Donald. Now we will be having peace and quietness in Bealtuinn. But you're not looking yourself at all. Man, but the influenza's a wicked thing right enough." He considered the wickedness of influenza for a moment. "I was passing Jimmy Robertson down the road. There is a fellow that is half dead this morning, aye a man that's left his coffin for a wee run round in the sunshine. A box of matches, Kenny, my boy." The stalker was in excellent form.

Kenny told him what Robertson had said. Grant slowly

packed his pipe. When he had lit up and filled the shop with smoke he said:

"Maybe he was after putting you off the scent. Is that what you're thinking too, Mr Blair? He's always been a fly little rascal, that Jimmy Robertson. Aye, wily as the Devil's own serpent. I'm thinking we'll be needing to stick eyes in the backs of our heads for the next few days."

"Days, John? You think they'll be back as soon as that?"

"Aye, Kenny, I'm thinking it's likely enough."

"I agree," said Gavin.

"You think he is in it then?"

"Aye, Donald, he is in it. Up to his bloody neck."

"Can we not be fixing him?" Kenny asked belligerently.

"Now, Kenny." Constable McPhail shook his head sadly. "Catch him, catch them all and bring them to me and I'll be charging them quick enough."

"Och, Donald man, it's not charging they're needing, it's this." Kenny held up a large fist. "What did they get away with the other night at Dualainn? Have you heard anything, John?"

"I was having a word with Dugald Macintyre and he was telling me he had only found two wounded beasts. The Lord knows how many they were killing, but they were getting away with the lot."

"Probably helped to recoup their losses."

"Maybe they'll stay over there," suggested Donald hopefully.

The stalker shook his head. "There's very few deer on Invershin."

"I have a cousin over in Dualainn," Kenny said. "You'll be remembering him, John? Donald Iain."

"The wee fellow with shoulders on him like a bull?"

"Aye, the very same. Well, he was telling me the night they had the poachers he was hearing two cars go by."

"Two?"

"Aye, Mr Blair, two."

"So they're expanding now. How the hell can they go driving about the countryside in a damned great fleet of cars. Hell, I don't know. Nobody seems to be able to do anything about it. Take this last do. No one heard anything, no shooting I mean. Well, that's understandable I suppose; if there's a wind blowing the wrong way they could use twenty-five pounders in some of these corries and you wouldn't hear a thing, not half a mile away. So no one disturbed them. They were able to drive in, shoot their deer, load them into their two vehicles and drive away, pleased as Punch with themselves. By now they'll have cashed in and have their pockets stuffed with fivers. Money for old rope, isn't it?" Gavin laughed sourly.

"They have plenty of places to choose from, Mr Blair," said Donald. "They can arrive here today and be poaching deer fifty miles away tomorrow night."

"Or they can vanish into thin air like they've done four times already. Remarkable."

Grant got out his turnip watch. "If we are going after this hummel, Mr Blair, we'd best be moving."

"You're getting him late in the season," said Donald.

"Aye, but he's a beast that needs shooting. He's limping badly. Maybe he was stopping one of them poaching bullets."

"Man, but I'd like to be out on the hill," broke in Kenny wistfully, "instead of hiding away in here among a lot of sweetie jars. Let me know if you'll be needing me," he called after them. "I'm handy enough with my fists. Or a rifle, if you're thinking of having a go at these fellows."

They heard his loud Viking laugh, and the voice of the policeman admonishing, "Now, Kenny."

* * * * *

They passed through the trees and out on to the southern flank of Beinn Gobhair. They climbed for a while and then stopped to spy from a heathery knoll. The day was very clear, free from haze, and visibility was excellent; but the winter sun held little warmth and the breeze roaming over the scattered stretches of soft snow was knife-edged. The stalker moved his glass slowly across the slope rising above them. Gavin watched an eagle circling with broad sweeps, and then turned his attention to the cold, glinting sea. A boat was passing across the entrance to the loch, heading north, well inshore, trailing a long white plume of gulls. He blew on his hands. It was too cold to hang about.

"See anything, John?"

"Aye, he's there. In the place I was seeing him yesterday. In a wee hollow just below Wolf Rock. He'll not be wanting to move, not with that leg on him." He handed over the glass. Gavin focused on the rock shaped like a sleeping wolf. There below it he picked up the hornless head of their quarry.

"Very pale head, almost white."

"Aye, he's like the silver stag we were going after last year. That fellow on the Big Sister. Man, but that was a stalk."

"How'll we go from here?"

"We'll go back to the trees and then round so's to come up to him from those broken peats. There are some old peat cuttings we can be using for the last three hundred yards. It shouldn't be difficult at all. There is no hurry. He will lie for a good while yet."

They sat out of the wind while the stalker smoked contentedly and Gavin watched the beetle progress of the boat. The afternoon sun was arching down towards the sea, touching the islands with pale fire. The days were drawing in; in another two hours it would be dark. Presently the two men retraced their steps, back into the trees. Hidden from watchful eyes on the mountain they kept to the wood till they could no longer see the Wolf Rock, then emerged once more into the open and began to climb in a long wide sweep so as to approach their animal across the broken slope and into the wind.

"We will have to be watching for hinds. They're popping up from nowhere in this place, quick as weasels."

At first the going was easy, no more than a slow stroll, then suddenly they were in full view of the rock, and the stalker signalled with his hand. They moved from cover to cover, crouching, often crawling on their stomachs along the sodden peat runnels and through the wet snow. The sun was full in their faces and behind the hummel; that at least was in his favour. But his hunters were skilled, using the ground expertly, inching flat as snakes across the open patches—very slowly, getting ever closer. The animal was sleepy; the pain in his foreleg, where the chip of shattered rock had torn a ragged wound, had eased to the dull throbbing of festered flesh. He moved his jaws in slow chewing rhythm, lying sheltered from the sea wind. Now and then little flurries curled round the rock but brought no hint of danger. Soon he would get up and feed. But not yet. At the moment he was drowsy and content. Once or twice he licked the blackened hole on the thigh of his leg.

Out in front his enemies lay planning how to get closer. Grant raised his head very gently, dropped back very slowly.

"Don't be moving now!" A hind was standing on a little rise staring full in their direction. For perhaps five minutes they lay pressed close to the slimy black peat. And not once did she take her eyes off them. Her ears were pricked; she advanced a few paces to a better vantage point. The stalker watched her through thin heather, never moving a muscle, except to hiss from the side of his mouth, "That's a suspicious bitch."

Satisfied there was no danger, her head went down. Slowly her back sank from view as she fed away from them. They continued their edging, crawling progress. But this time they were moving backwards. They reached a high bank and straightened up behind it.

"He'll be lying there for a wee while."

Grant lit his pipe. Gavin peered cautiously round the bank.

"About a hundred and fifty, isn't he?"

"Aye, thereabouts. The light's going a wee bit. You'll not be needing too much foresight."

Out of the wind it was very quiet, very still and very peaceful. A fat heather spider made its way up the canvas cover of the rifle. Gavin saw the half-past-two ferry cutting its broad wake across the loch. In an hour and a half the sun that was shining red and green from the tin roofs of Rappoch would be touching the sea. He wondered what his wife was doing and hoped she was not getting too tired. Then he drew the rifle from its cover and slid a round gently into the breech. The blue steel shone dully with the sheen of oil. It was a beautiful piece of work. He remembered the Minister's words. ". . . An instrument of great kindness . . . or of great pain and suffering . . ." He turned it over in his hands, brought the butt into his cheek, aiming at the roof of the Manse. Beside him the stalker stirred and took a look over the top.

"He's lying. We'll give him a wee bit longer then we'll have to be getting him up ourselves." At that moment a grouse left the heather and flew whirring and shouting its alarm, straight past the rock.

"He's up!"

Gavin raised the Mannlicher slowly over the lip of the bank.

"Take him now!"

The hummel was broadside, a perfect shot.

"He'll not be waiting long."

Grass waved across the sights. Gavin shifted the rifle and light must have glinted on the barrel. The animal snorted, turned swiftly and made off up the hillside.

"Hell!"

"He'll maybe stop for a moment on the skyline."

Sure enough the animal paused just below the crest and turned to look back. The high-velocity bullet took him clean through the edge of the pumping heart. He did not fall but ran strongly out of sight.

Gavin felt the stalker's hand clapping him on the shoulder. "Well done. Well done. He'll not be going far, that one. He was dead when the bullet struck him." They scrambled over the rocky scree and found the hummel stone-dead in the snow on the summit.

"A big beast right enough. Sixteen stone, I'm thinking, never a pound less. There's not a stag in the forest that could be standing up to this fellow." The stalker lifted the foreleg.

"Aye, he was hit before all right."

He removed his jacket and got out his long-bladed knife. Gavin sat to watch the expert cleaning of the dead animal. A big brute of a hummel too. Having no antlers to drain his strength, a hummel will often grow to a great size. In battle he fights with his feet and few horned stags will face his ferocity and weight.

"I have seen this fellow here with more than eighty hinds all to himself. Och, he was a greedy beggar. He's better out of the way." Grant drew out the grey bag of the stomach. He plunged his hands back inside the great rent in the belly and pulled forth the various delicacies: kidneys, liver and then the smashed heart. He laid them neatly in a row, bloody prizes in the snow. His massive arms were red to the elbow. The rest of the viscera he threw in a palpitating heap. Gavin watched and thought, 'Who am I to talk of cruelty? But at least this animal died cleanly and quickly—and surely that is all any man or beast can ask: a quick and painless death'. Yet he need not have killed at all. That was true; he need not. He plucked a piece of grass and began to chew. The stalker took the tripe and filled the whitish sack with the delicacies, popping them in one by one as though dropping coins into a bag. A few minutes ago this animal lived and breathed, now it's a mess of flesh and bone and ugly remains. Gavin spat out the grass. Why don't you take photographs of them? That's what Margaret always asked. Why do you have to kill them? And to that he could never find any good answer. But at least they did not suffer. That was always his excuse. To inflict quick death is excusable, to inflict suffering is not. Is that it?

"I'll be going for the pony," said the stalker, wiping his arms with a handful of wet moss. "Would you be staying here till I get back, or coming down with me, Mr Blair?"

"I'll stay."

He thrust aside the dark thoughts. Four ravens had appeared, sensing death in the same uncanny way as vultures. They alighted one by one on nearby rocks and perched, stretching out their hideous heads, opening their devilish beaks in silent gloating.

"It'll not be taking me long."

Grant swung away downhill with the long strides of a man born to the mountains. Gavin watched him go. Beyond his large stooping figure he saw the boat very clearly in a beam of sunshine lancing through the gathering clouds. He took the glass from the case and brought the boat close to his eyes. There was something about the build of her, the way she butted through the rising swell——

"John, it's her! It's the boat that tried to sink us." He was on his feet pointing. Picking up the rifle he ran down the hill.

"They're heading for Glenaila. I'm damned sure they are. We've got to get back. Now, at once."

"Now steady, Mr Blair. Even if they are taking the channel through the Knucklebones they cannot be reaching Glenaila not for a good half-hour. If that is where they are going," he added dubiously.

"Perhaps not. It may not even be the same boat, but we can't take a chance on it, John. Not after last time. Will you drive me back?"

"Aye, Mr Blair, surely." They hurried towards the trees.

"If that is the same boat, then I'm thinking the poaching lads'll be back tonight again. From the sea maybe or the land —or both." He raised his face to the strengthening breeze.

"There's more wind coming tonight. They'll not be finding it easy to land, not in the swell that'll soon be running."

Gavin was hardly listening. He was thinking of Margaret alone at the farm.

"Look at that!" exclaimed Grant. "She's not fancying the Knucklebones." The boat was veering seawards to pass outside the rocks.

"Thank God!" said Gavin. He took one last look at the boat crawling steadily over the blood-red sea before they entered the trees. On the path he began to run, consumed by impatience and fear for his wife.

[10]

MARGARET was on the shore with Pusan and Chiquita when the boat came round the Knucklebones. As soon as she saw it heading into the bay with a man standing in the bows with field-glasses to his eyes, she too knew the boat. But she remained where she was, pretending to rummage in the seaweed, covertly watching as the yawl slowly approached the pier. She knew her face would be clearly seen by the man in the bows and hoped her expression was sufficiently casual to hide the unpleasant bumping of her heart. Calling to Chiquita she turned her steps slowly and calmly towards the house. The calf ran and splashed in the little pools, loving the game but, as always, disgusted by the salt on her nose and coat.

The man still watched from the bows. He had been joined by a figure in yellow oilskins. By now Margaret could make out the deep *chug-chug-chug* of the idling engine. They appeared to be in no hurry. Perhaps she was mistaken; perhaps they were only fishermen. But she knew they were not and wished she was not alone. At the house she glanced back to where the boat squatted on the lazy swell, black and sinister in the eye of the setting sun. She felt the first stirring of the wind in her hair. If only it would blow up quickly as it often did on these still days, then they'd never be able to land.

"Chiquita!" The calf was dawdling, snuffling at the sand. Margaret called again. "Come on, can't you." Any moment the boat might put in to the pier.

What had they come back for? What could she do with only the dog to help her? She remembered the killing of the rams and the ruthless way that same boat had tried to sink them. There was Gavin's old rifle, the one in the cupboard under the stairs. He had shown her how to shoot; she could at least aim the thing.

"Chiquita! For goodness' sake, come *on*!"

The little animal skipped about happily. The men had vanished from the deck. The swell was still long and lazy, no obstacle to a big boat; there was nothing to stop it coming in, landing the men and then waiting off-shore to pick them up after . . . after what? Margaret grabbed the protesting calf by the collar and dragged her into the house. She locked the doors and snibbed the windows; then she got the rifle, loaded it with three bullets, all she could find, and posted herself by the drawing-room window where she could cover the pier and the path to the house. She waited for what might happen.

Presently the man in the oilskins reappeared, this time holding a boat-hook. The yawl turned in a tight arc across the swell, heading for the pier. Margaret opened the window a few inches and poked out the muzzle of the rifle; she gripped the weapon so tightly that the knuckles of her small hands showed white; her heart thumped and her inside went empty as a vacuum.

They were definitely coming in now, riding high over the swell. Two men in the bows, one holding a coiled rope. The boat edged towards the pier and the man with the rope crouched ready to jump. Margaret pushed forward the safety catch. Please, God, don't let me hit anyone. Just let me frighten them out of their wits, that's all. At the first attempt the man failed to jump and the boat turned sharply away to make another attempt. Back it came, closer, closer. A man was signalling with his arm. The skipper put her close as he dared and this time the man leapt for the shore, landing in a sprawling heap. Frightened of the swell, the skipper veered away and, as he did so, Margaret's finger jerked convulsively at the trigger. The crash of the shot in the room deafened her, the kick of the heavy rifle bruised her shoulder. The bullet smacked into the crest of a dark green swell, sending up a little plume of spray. At the sound the man on the pier spun round facing the house in time to see the smoke of the next shot and hear the crack of the bullet past his head. He flung himself flat on his face.

This second bullet had gone very much closer to the boat than Margaret had intended; so close, in fact, that it severed the forestay with an angry twang. The man in the oilskins disappeared like a shot rabbit. Without waiting for more, the skipper put the wheel hard over and headed for the open sea, deaf to the shouts from the man stranded on the pier.

"Och, shut your bloody mouth!" He wasn't going in there again to have his boat sunk under him by some madman. He hadn't wanted to come back at all, but the money had been good. With the fishing being so poor and him with four hungry mouths to feed, well, a man was having to take what he could get. But he was not risking his boat, not in the sea that was running, not for any bloody poachers. He opened the throttle wide. He would not be happy till there was a lot of water between himself and that wicked shore.

Back on the pier the man got to his feet. Nothing happened. He took a few tentative steps up the path to the house. Still nothing happened. Then a woman's voice ordered him to stop.

"Stay where you are. I warn you, I'll shoot."

The man stopped in his tracks.

"You wouldn't, you know," he called.

"Just you try."

He took out a grubby white handkerchief and raised it above his head.

"All right, lady. I know when I'm beat. O.K., lady, *kamarad*." He came slowly forward again, watching the figure in the open window.

"Stop. I tell you, I'll shoot. Stop where you are."

She found she was shaking like a leaf, but managed to keep her voice calm.

"Now what would you want to be doing that for, lady?

What are you playing at, eh? A bloke comes ashore for some matches and gets shot at. I ask you, lady, is that polite?"

As he talked, so he advanced towards the house, waving his handkerchief. He saw the rifle come up and jumped for cover behind a little hillock beside the path just as she fired the last round. He mopped his forehead. Christ, she meant business all right! He heard the slam of the window, then the sound of a car drawing up beyond the house. Margaret was at the telephone when she heard it too, then running feet and Gavin's urgent voice.

"Margaret, where are you? Are you all right? Margaret?" He rattled the back door. They had spotted the boat as the car rounded the Big Sister. John thought he had heard a shot. Gavin beat at the door with his fist.

"Where are you?" The key turned, the door opened and she was in his arms.

"Oh, darling, I'm glad you're back." She clung to him for a moment, her face in his shoulder, while he stroked her hair.

"There's a man hiding by the path. He thinks I'm going to shoot him, he's waving a white handkerchief, and says he wants matches. The boat put him ashore. I think there were more of them but they cleared off. Oh, Gavin, I thought I'd hit the captain, the boat did such odd things and——"

"Hit the captain? Margaret, you haven't been shooting at them?" Astonishment struggled with admiration on his face and in his voice.

"Only three shots, darling, that was all."

Admiration won.

"Well, you're quite a woman, you really are." Admiration gave way to amusement and he burst out laughing, holding her away from him, his hands on her shoulders.

"I didn't aim at them. But I thought if you were able to frighten them then perhaps I could."

"Good lord, I should think so! That rifle's about twice as big as you are to start with. Frighten them! That boat won't stop till it gets to New York." He kissed her soundly on the lips.

"I have a fellow here, Mr Blair, I'm thinking you will want to be asking a few questions," said Grant as he came round the corner of the house. "I was noticing him trying to creep away behind the byres there." Beside him stood a small thin man with the expression of a scared and sullen rat.

"Well," said Gavin coldly. "What were you after this time?"

"I've no idea what ye mean, mister." He spoke with the accent of Glasgow.

"He's saying he came ashore to ask for matches. I was telling him he'll be needing to think up a better one than that."

"It's the truth," spat Rat Face. "We run out."

"Have you been here before?" Gavin asked.

"Never."

"Why did your friends leave you like that?"

"We was shot at by this—this——"

"Careful," said Gavin. His look was dangerous.

"This lady here."

"Last time anyone came here by boat they killed two of my rams. But you won't know anything about that. Will you?"

"Why should I? I tell you, I never seen this place before. And I hope I never sees it again."

"You won't, don't worry."

Gavin's tone brought a quick flicker of alarm to the man's eyes.

"Look here, Jock," he began truculently.

"My name is not Jock."

"We should be taking him to Donald," suggested the stalker. "It will be dark in about an hour and we'll need to be thinking what's to be done."

"Yes, I think Constable McPhail will be very interested in one or two small things."

"He'll be interested enough when I tell him I been shot at." Rat Face rounded on Margaret. "I'll hae the law on ye for what ye did."

"Will you?" she answered sweetly. "What fun!"

"Come on," interrupted Gavin briskly. "We haven't time to argue now. John, you'd better take him along to Donald. We'll nip over to Famista and see if we can get hold of Captain Downie."

"Ye'll no get awa' wi' this." Rat Face scowled at them.

"And would you be trying to stop us, you miserable little rascal?" inquired the stalker quietly. The man swore nastily under his breath but did not answer.

"I'll get the car." Margaret ran to the garage.

"Try to get hold of Kenny, John. And if he's coming with us he'd better put on something warm and bring some sort of a weapon. Meet you at the shop soon as we can. All right?"

The stalker nodded. He jerked his thumb at his car.

"Inside, wee man, and don't you be trying anything, mind."

The man hesitated.

"Am I needing to help you in?" Grant took a step forward.

Rat Face scrambled into the car.

"See you at the shop," said Gavin.

"Aye, Mr Blair, I'll be joining you just as soon as I can."

* * * * *

The four of them were gathered in Mrs Carmichael's little sitting-room at the back of the shop: Gavin and Margaret, Mike Downie and Kenny. They sipped at Mrs Carmichael's tea and nibbled at her rock cakes, waiting for John's return from the policeman's house. Gavin looked at his watch for the tenth time.

"He's being a long time over it." Restless and impatient, he went to the window. The sun was setting behind the islands, sinking into a blaze of molten glory. Snow clouds were banking thick in the north-west and he could see the wind rushing in sudden fierce squalls across the waters of the loch.

"It'll be pitch dark in about half an hour. Ah, that's him." Heavy steps sounded in the shop. "Evening, John. What news from the police front?"

"Good evening, Captain. Well, Donald is trying to telephone the Inspector in Fort Henry. But I'm thinking the line was not good at all. He was having to shout terrible loud to get the number."

"What about the man?" asked Margaret.

"Och, he was still blethering away about his rights and saying he could not be kept there, he had not been doing anything wrong. Och, a lot of rubbish. Donald was telling him to hold his noise and wait till the Inspector came. And Donald was saying, 'John,' he was saying, 'you'll not be doing anything on your own now, you'll be waiting for the police this time,' he was saying. 'We'll not be having any more shootings and chasings in the dark.' "

"Good grief!" roared Mike. "We can't hang about waiting for the law to catch up. We'll be here all ruddy night. A time for the Nelson touch, a bit of the old blind eye, eh, Gavin?"

Gavin glanced up from the map on the table and nodded.

"So we're getting a chance at these fellows quicker than we thought," said Kenny joyfully. He was already dressed for action, in a short heavy jacket, corduroy trousers tied at the knees, and huge nailed boots. He carried a short heavy stick.

"If they turn up." Mike was in great fettle at the prospect of a scrap; arrayed in a strange assortment of ex-army garments: sweaters and khaki scarf and camouflage smock; on his head a greasy stocking cap. By his chair lay a steel-shafted golf club. "Thought I'd bring the old bundook, but we don't want a ruddy massacre. Brought the number seven mashie in lieu, ha-ha. Does for golf balls or heads, doesn't matter."

"They'll be coming," answered Kenny confidently. "Aye, they'll be coming all right." He smacked the stick softly against his open palm. The Viking eyes were merry. His mother brought in the lamps and drew the curtains against the coming night. A flurry of sleety snow struck against the window.

"I am not envying you," she said.

"We'll be all right, Mother. Don't you be worrying yourself."

"What's the form, old boy?" Mike turned to Gavin. They all turned to Gavin, Margaret noticed, but without surprise. He seemed to take complete charge, quite quietly, no fuss, no shouting. For all Mike's size and shrewdness and experience, it was Gavin who took command. She sat in the armchair and listened proudly to her husband's plan.

Mike and Kenny would go to the summit of Creag Dhu and there wait developments.

"It seems the best observation post in the whole area."

"Agreed," said Mike. Kenny nodded.

"You may be up there one hour, six hours, the whole night, I don't know. All I do know is, it'll be damned cold."

"That'll not be killing us, Mr Blair."

He and Margaret would come into the Glen of the Skull by way of the Chasm.

"Good for you, Margaret," Mike boomed. "Still, this'll be nothing after taking on their ruddy navy."

She flushed slightly and smiled. But Gavin was worried. These men were tough and dangerous and certainly no respecters of women who got in the way. He had tried to tell her she should not come, that she should stay with Mrs Carmichael and the animals. But . . . He glanced across the room at her. She was excited as a child, he could see that, but quite calm and composed, sitting there quietly in her leather sheepskin jacket and little tweed trousers. She caught his look and smiled the smile she reserved for him. In spite of his anxiety he was very happy she would be with him.

On their way round to the Wailing Loch they would drop

the stalker and he would make his way down the Black Burn to the big rowan tree below the waterfall, where he, too, would wait developments.

"Splitting the forces badly, I know, but it's the only possible way of covering the ground. Whoever runs into them first will just have to cope according to the situation." Murmurs of agreement.

"Of course, if they come and decide to go to Sgurr Gheal or the Flats, well," he shrugged, "then we've had it."

"Most of the deer are on the west of the road," said Grant. "If Jimmy Robertson is with them, then I'm thinking the little devils will be trying along the top of Skull Glen."

The squalls were following each other with increasing rapidity, booming in the chimney, blowing puffs of smoke into the room.

"It is a terrible night," said Mrs Carmichael, looking at Margaret and shaking her head.

"Just the night they'll be wanting, Mother."

"It's time we were moving," said Gavin. He folded the map. "Is everyone clear on the plan?"

"How shall we be knowing each other in the dark, Mr Blair?"

"Good point, Kenny." Gavin thought for a moment. "Have we all got torches." All had. "What about short-long repeated? All right?"

Yes. There were no further questions. They went out into the stormy evening. It was already getting dark.

"Be careful, Kenny lad," said his mother.

"He'll be all right, Mrs C. Not to worry." Mike patted the old woman on the arm. Chiquita stood in the lighted doorway to see them off; Pusan barked and tugged at his leash, frantic at being left behind by the departing car.

The hills had the dark, flat look of dusk; for the moment the wind had dropped to a breeze, but it was bitterly cold and thin snow fell on them as they stood by the car at Hump Bridge.

A few last whispered questions and instructions, then Mike and Kenny faded into the darkness, the former jabbing enthusiastically at the sky with his thumb. Farther on Gavin dropped the stalker and he, too, vanished into the long cleft of the Black Burn.

Gavin and Margaret left the car in the little quarry beside the road and followed the path round the shore of the Wailing Loch. As they got into the lee of the Big Sister the night became suddenly very still save for the splash of water on the bleached rocks. But as they reached the entrance to the Chasm another shower enveloped them in blustering greyness. They huddled in the miserable shelter of the birch trees. Above them the skeleton branches whipped madly in the wind and all the fiends of hell played round them, shrieking and moaning in that tormented place. It seemed to Margaret that devilish laughter rang through the storm—grief, rage and a wild mockery. A witches' song rising from the inky waters of the loch. She pressed close to her husband, shivering at the sound. He put his arm round her shoulder and his mouth close to her ear:

"The wind. That's all."

With a final long-drawn wail the storm rushed away, quickly as it had come, leaving ragged clouds through which the moon showed very bright.

"All right?" he asked.

She nodded, clenching her small hands, quite speechless from the cold.

"We'll go as far as the shieling, then wait."

Clutching her stick tightly she followed close. Together they entered between the towering walls of the ravine.

* * * * *

Along the edges of the road between Creag Dhu and the white mass of Beinn Mhor the deer had been scraping away the shallow snow since dusk to reach the grass below. All along the Black Burn they had been grazing, placid and unsuspicious, not bothering about the snow showers which drove hard against their coats. Occasionally one of the hinds would throw up her head to sniff the bitter air. Whenever the wind dropped you could hear the crunch and crackle of neat little hooves in the crusted patches of snow, and the scrape of them on rock. Down by the sea a few deer skirted the Quaking Sands, looking for seaweed on the high-tide line.

The black stag fed with his small shadow, the two of them grazing slowly into the Glen of the Skull. They found little grass, and what they did uncover was coarse and brittle. Though they moved among the shadowy shapes of many deer they did not join others but fed alone, proud and aloof. Hidden by the snow showers they felt reasonably secure, but when the moon lit up the land with the touch of pale daylight and the ground was starkly black and white, then the calf grew restless. It would eat a mouthful, then up with its head to stare suspiciously, the moonlight shining in the soft, anxious eyes. The little animal became more and more restless, till it did not lower its head at all but stood stock-still staring into the shadows. After a while everything became too much for the calf and it gave a snort of alarm, running a few yards, stiff-legged like a toy deer. The stag raised his head. Grass hung from his mouth which went on chewing. But the calf snorted again and this time ran to him, nudging his flank, warning him to run from danger while there was still time.

And the stag paid heed and followed his small companion, and together they made off down the slope of Creag Dhu into the glen below.

* * * * *

Kenny kept close to the Captain, but was hardly seeing him for the swirling white murk of the storm. He was hardly seeing where to put his feet, but stumbled on, head bent, excited as a schoolboy on an escapade. His life as storekeeper in Rappoch was not conspicuous for incident or adventure; a fortnightly trip to Fort Henry; an occasional Saturday afternoon at the fishing, that was all. The wind howled round his numbed ears, lashed the snow against his face, but he did not care. He did not care about anything save that he'd been chosen to accompany them. He wiped the snow from his eyes, grinning to himself.

From the top of Creag Dhu they looked down the glen, right to the silvery bar of the sea. The Black Burn snaked through the white wastes; the mountains glistened with strange, unearthly brilliance and the shadows were black as sin. Mike held up his hand in the sudden stillness following the storm.

"What's that?"

Something clattered on the rocks far below. With his glasses he could just make out the dim shapes slipping from view across the snow.

"Deer."

He thumped his arms against his sides. "Good grief, it's brass monkeys up here. Hope we don't get another of those ruddy showers. A gang of ruddy elephants could have gone by in that last one and you couldn't have heard a thing."

He was quite right. At the first onset of the squall, while they were pushing slowly up the slope, a big estate car and a van had come over Hump Bridge from the direction of Fort Henry, moving at a crawl and guided by a man walking in front, a man who knew every bump and curve in the road. Unseen and unheard, the poachers had come secretly into the Forest. They concealed the vehicles behind the broken wall of the tumbledown sheep-fank at Piper's Croft. Sheltered by the mountain, they prepared themselves for what they hoped would be their last and most successful slaughter. There were three of them, who loaded their weapons and striped their faces with soot in the way of soldiers going on patrol. They did not speak, and except for a brief flash of a torch did nothing to reveal their presence. The leader consulted the luminous hands of his watch and glanced frequently into the lifting storm. As soon as he saw patches of moonlit sky through the racing clouds he gave a signal with his upraised arm.

The three men moved round the northern shoulder of Creag Dhu and into the Glen of the Skull, leaving a man to watch the vehicles.

[11]

John Grant knew the ways of the wind in Skull Glen as well as he knew his deer; he knew the mischievous little swirl of it by the big rowan tree and how any deer feeding this end of the glen would likely be getting the wind of him as soon as he crossed the burn. He went across the stepping-stones below the waterfall with the water round his boots, and along the burnside till he reached the tree. Then he uttered a high piercing whistle. Away in front, at the far edge of the moonlight, a large party of deer threw up their heads. He flicked his torch on and off, hit the tree sharply with his stick and clapped his hands. As usual it was a hind that came forward peering short-sightedly towards danger. She stamped her forefoot in alarm, then turned and went away fast, taking the others with her in a long streaming bunch. Grant heard them go and smiled with satisfaction. That was one lot away out of it.

The wind came tearing up the great funnel of the glen, rattling sleet in the branches. He moved to the sheltered side of the tree and waited for the shower to pass. The tree-trunk moved hard against his back. Maybe they'll not be coming at all, he thought. Or maybe they'll be trying another part of the Forest altogether. He had spent many long hours of his life waiting in the darkness; often wet, often cold. But now he was getting old. Tonight he was feeling his age and feeling the damned pain in his back; he was feeling the cold and thinking of his bed. Aye, that was the only way to be stopping the ache, flat on his back with a mattress below him. He moved irritably. And all for a wee piece of Jerry steel all those years back. Och, well, you're not lying out there in the Salient. You're still alive, man. He hoped very much they would be coming tonight. Man alive, but he would be liking a proper crack at them. Just once before he left Bealtuinn. This would be his last season, aye, there was no doubt of that at all. He was not fit for the hill any more, he knew that. The rushing roar of the swollen burn was very loud and he felt the spray of the waterfall on his face. The sound made him drowsy; he closed his eyes, pressing hard against the tree to still the nagging pain in his back.

Something roused him. Some instinct, that sixth sense possessed by men who are hunters and watchers. The storm had passed and the night was clear. Something was moving. He could see nothing, but he knew they were there. He shut his eyes for a second, opened them to bright moonlight. Two figures were visible against the milky white waterfall, picking their way gingerly across the stones. He crouched back into the shadow of the tree, longing for his rifle. One—two—three of them. He could have bowled them over easy as rabbits and them not knowing what had hit them. And he with nothing but a silly wee stick! On the near bank they stopped and huddled for a moment, then came on down the deer path, moving slowly. The leading man paused by the tree, so close the stalker could have been on him in a couple of strides. Grant knew that man well enough; he'd be knowing him anywhere with that way of holding his head. So now he was seeing the little bastard with his own eyes. The dirty little rascal!

They moved on again and he saw that Jimmy Robertson was carrying a tommy gun in the crook of his arm. The next man had a bulky thing on his back, some sort of a pack, and the third man held a service rifle at the ready. Their faces were streaky black, like bloody zebras they were. They were well-spaced, he noticed with grudging approval, but the last fellow was not knowing his job. He was never once looking over his shoulder, not once.

Grant allowed them to the very limit of his sight before stepping from the shadows and following in their footsteps.

A sudden gust blew snow in his face, then it was gone and in its place a dim and cloudy darkness. He cursed the dullness of his ears, him that could be hearing a worm breathe not so long ago, and his eyes watered with the strain of trying to make out the men ahead. The farther they were going into the glen the better, for then they'd have them trapped. But they would not be going too far from the road, not with Jimmy leading them. Shielding his torch, he flashed towards the summit of Creag Dhu, short-long, short-long. Maybe the Captain or Kenny would be spotting it and coming down to help.

With no scrap of warning the blazing spotlight split the darkness in front. Deer stood at the end of the long beam, not moving. A voice rapped out, "Fire!" and the night was hideously torn by the racket of a sub-machine gun and rifle. ·303 tracer bullets streaked along the beam and climbed as red sparks into the darkness. Grant heard the clatter of the magazine being changed, then the tommy gun was firing again. He saw only two animals go down before the rest broke and ran. He, too, was running, shouting with all his powerful lungs.

"Captain! Kenny!" A torch winked from the hillside and he heard a mighty hallooing from the Captain. The spotlight went out, leaving the night suddenly very dark. Men were calling to each other close in front.

"Heh," he roared. "You there!"

The answer came with a bright whipcrack that cut the air past his head.

"There's something to take 'ome. And 'ere's another!" The second tracer went wide, ricocheting in a slow red curve up the mountain face. Grant did not stop, nor even hesitate. He was filled with a blazing anger. He heard Jimmy Robertson urging them to come on and run for it. That dirty little swine, using a bloody machine gun on the deer, and him a man brought up as a stalker.

"Just you be letting me get my hands on you, James Robertson." The stalker tried to increase speed, but the pain of his old wound took him suddenly and he had to stop, winded and gasping and bent helpless. A fresh shower swept up the glen, drowning the noise of the poachers and covering their escape.

By the time Mike and Kenny reached him Grant had recovered his breath.

"All right, John?" They stood with their backs to the shower.

"Aye. But I was letting them get away and them so close at one moment I could have spat and hit the little devils. Three of them, led by that Robertson."

"Which way did they go?"

"Down the glen, towards the sea."

"They may make a break for it through the Chasm."

"I'm hoping not, Captain. There's one bastard among them that was firing at me. Twice. Tracer bullets. I would not like Mrs Blair to be getting mixed up with such dangerous fellows."

"I know. I agree. One of those bullets came pretty close to us."

"Aye," put in Kenny excitedly. "Right between us it went. Another foot either way and one of us would have been getting it right enough. Are we not going after them?" His blood was up.

"Not in this. We'd not be seeing a yard before our faces."

They sheltered in the lee of a peat-hag.

"The murdering swine," Kenny kept repeating. Mike considered what to do when the storm lifted. If they went on they might catch up, but unlikely. Besides, there was nothing to stop the poachers lying up till they'd gone past, then nipping back to the road and the vehicles. That's what he'd do in their shoes. Better get back to the road, nab the transport and wait for the brutes to show up. Pull all the leads out, that'd fix 'em, or let the tyres down. They'd be properly scuppered then. Yes, that's the plan. The shower lasted for about ten minutes, then slackened to scattered snowflakes. Mike put forward his idea. Kenny was all for going on. John thought the plan sound enough but said they should go on to the Chasm.

"If the poachers are going that way, then Mr Blair will be needing us, Captain."

"I'll go on," Mike decided firmly. "You two get back to the road and find their ruddy van and put it out of action. But watch it, they've probably left a bloke to look after the thing. Good grief, John, I'll be all right. I can look after myself. Cheer up, Kenny m'lad. You're just as likely to get a crack at 'em as I am."

He waited till they were out of sight, then started along the burn path very slowly, often stopping to look and listen, slipping from one patch of shadow to the next, moving with all the stealth and skill of a hunting animal, enjoying himself; for this was something Mike Downie was really good at.

* * * * *

The sound of the distant shots was picked up and magnified by the steep sides of the Chasm. From the shieling they had seen the glow of the spotlight in the sky just before the darkness of the storm descended on the Chasm. They were quite sheltered where they waited. When the shower had passed Gavin told his wife to stay back out of sight while he stood by the corner of the wall watching the path along which the poachers might come. This time, he said to himself, surely this time. He never took his eyes off the sharp bar of shadow flung across the path some fifty yards up the moonlit ravine. It was half-past five. If nothing happened by six they would go to the end of the Chasm. At least they knew the poachers were in the Forest. The shots had seemed to come from the direction of Beinn Mhor, but it could have been farther, beyond the river. He wondered what the hell was happening. He strained his ears; only the steady sigh of the wind. He strained his eyes; only the black and white ravine where nothing moved. No more shots. He moved restlessly, wondering if they were wasting their time. They might be needed. He felt out of things. The poachers might have got away yet again. Clouds swept across the moon. He called to Margaret and she joined him.

"Doesn't look as if anyone's coming this way. We'd better go on, I think, and see if anything's happening in the glen."

"Sst!" She held her head on one side. "I heard something. I'm sure I heard something."

He motioned her back behind the wall. The moon reappeared, casting the same black shadow across the path. Gavin heard the clink and rattle of stones. He watched the sharp black edge and tensed himself, ready to spring.

Out from the bar of blackness came a stag, then another, and a third. A long file of beasts made their way along the track, silvery pale in the moonlight, stepping cautiously. One by one they passed the watchers by the shieling, the breath steamy at their nostrils, their eyes glinting now and then in the light of the near full moon. Twenty-three stags moving quite silently but for the occasional small sounds of their hooves on stones sticking through the shallow snow. And every one so close he could have scratched their ears with the end of his stick. The last one disappeared, fading beyond the range of human eyes.

"Oh," whispered Margaret rapturously. "Oh, darling, that was the most wonderful thing I've ever seen."

"Those stags hadn't been shot at, that's certain." Gavin looked at the scudding clouds. Wind north-west. They must have come round from Beinn Bhreac direction. Therefore the poachers, if they were in Skull Glen that is, must still be on the road side of the Chasm.

"We'll move," he said. "Keep close. If I stop, then you stop; if I drop, then you drop, see? Don't wait for me to tell you, just do what I do."

She nodded.

"And if we do run into them, for God's sake don't go trying anything on your own. If anyone comes for you, hit him across the throat. Like this." He chopped back-handed. "Or use your stick across his eyes."

This time she nodded uncertainly.

"Forget your kind heart. It's either him or you."

"Yes."

He squeezed her shoulder and kissed her on the forehead. "It'll be all right, love."

But they reached the end of the Chasm without further incident.

The Glen of the Skull stretched away either side, stark and pitiless in the cold moon-wash. Margaret had never seen the place so sinister, so glaring white and yet so full of shadow. From the corner of her eye she seemed to see the little corners of darkness move, yet when she looked quickly all was still and frozen. The sound of the swollen burn was very loud and the wind which came from the sea flayed her skin and burrowed to her bones. Something moved again. She turned her head sharply and this time the shadow did not vanish but came towards them, the dark shape of a man. She pulled at Gavin's arm, pointing up the path. At first he pushed her behind him, then relaxed and said:

"It's all right, it's Mike."

Back came the answering flash of the torch: short-long, short-long. Mike joined them.

"See anything?"

"They didn't come down the Chasm. A party of stags, that's all."

"They didn't double back for the road either. I'd have seen 'em. Course they may have lain doggo till I was past, then nipped back. That's what I'd have done. Still, not to worry, they'll run into John and Kenny." He explained. "Nobble the transport and we've got 'em on toast."

"What was the shooting?" asked Margaret.

"They took a crack at some deer at the far end of the glen. Then John went for them and broke up the party. We'd have got 'em if that ruddy shower hadn't bitched things. Question is, which way now? By God, we're not going to lose 'em this time." He swiped at the snow with his golf club.

"Listen," exclaimed Margaret, "what was that?" They listened. The rush of the burn; the distant roar of the sea; the wind swooping up the glen : that was all they heard.

"There it is again."

"You've got ruddy good ears, Margaret."

"She's right," said Gavin. "Someone's shouting."

Faint but unmistakable on the wind there came a cry. What could have been a cry of pain, of anger perhaps, but a definite human cry.

"Good grief, yes. Well done, Maggie. That's the way they've gone." They heard it again, agonised, imploring. "Someone's in trouble, that's ruddy certain. By God, d'you think it's the Sands?"

"We'd better get down there and find out."

They set off quickly down the glen towards the sea, but heard no more cries. The sky was very clear for a spell when they reached the shore and the ruins stood tumbled and bleached as piled bones; the windows of the cottage stared as black, sightless eyes from the moonlit walls. The Quaking Sands lay silent and motionless under the moon. Only the sea moved. They cast about like hounds that have lost a scent. Gavin wondered if the cries had been in their imaginations. Some seabirds maybe, or a trick of the wind. So they'd lost them again. Nothing for it but to make back to the road and hope that John and Kenny had had more luck. The sky darkened swiftly, snow swirled round them. They took shelter behind the cottage till the shower had passed. Mike stuck his head through a broken window, withdrew it sharply.

"Good grief, what a ruddy awful pong! There must be about fifty dead sheep in there."

They went round to the front. Gavin wondered what to do. Now and then thin spray struck him in the face from the pounding sea. He felt a pull at his arm. Margaret was pointing at the ground. There at his feet lay a cap.

So that was why they couldn't open the door. The poachers were barricaded in the cottage.

"Nothing here," he shouted loud above the surge of the sea, jerking with his head, drawing Mike's attention to the tell-tale cap. The latter was quick.

"Reckon they've headed back to the road," he shouted in answer.

"We'd better get after 'em."

"Yes."

They moved out of sight of the windows and into the comparative darkness of the ruins.

"By God!" said Mike. "So the brutes are in there. Why don't we rush 'em? You take one door, I'll take the other. Put the ruddy ferrets in and flush 'em out."

Gavin thought rapidly. There were at least three of them in the cottage. They were armed and they were cornered and very dangerous. He knew the sort of men they were up against. If he and Mike got knocked out, and it was on the cards, that left Margaret. He hesitated. All they had to do was keep them there till morning. By then the vehicles should be out of action.

"What are we waiting for?" Mike smacked the golf club against his open palm.

"We'd never get in. They'll only come out if they want to." He made up his mind. "Stay here," he said, and walked out across the moonlit grass towards the cottage.

Inside, two of the three men crouched, each beside a window, peering out. The third man, Jimmy Robertson, lay moaning with the pain of a badly broken shin. His foot had slipped down between two rocks as he ran, snapping the bone neat as you please. Now when he moved his body the protruding ends of bone scraped together like grinding teeth and brought the sweat to his grey face and the groans of agony bubbling from his throat. Beside him, so close he could touch them lay the rotting, crawling carcases of two long-dead sheep. The men held handkerchiefs to their faces against the filthy stench. Scrap, the vicious little man whose finger was so ready on the trigger, had wanted to leave the injured man and run for it.

"Nothing'll 'appen to 'im. They'll shove 'im in 'ospital, that's all. Come on, let's scarper. We can telephone and let 'em know where to find 'im." But the leader had refused.

"I'm in charge and I say we'll stay." So they had hauled him the last couple of hundred yards, stuffing his mouth with a gag to stifle the shrieks of pain. They barricaded the rickety door of the cottage, posted themselves at the windows and watched the grass, the dark ruins and the mountainous white swell rolling far up the shore. When the shower came they ducked down from the windows, letting the snow whirl above them. So they did not see their pursuers till the squall had gone. But Scrap, back at his window, swore he'd seen figures melting into the shadows of the ruins.

"I tell you I did. Two of 'em. They're 'ere. Over by that pile of stones. What'll we do, guv? Make a break for it?"

Robertson flung his head from side to side, biting back the red-hot pain of his shattered leg. The leader glanced at him.

"No. We'll stay put. They don't know we're here. We'll give them half an hour, then——"

"Another 'arf an hour? In this muckin' stink. Not muckin' likely. Not for me." Scrap's stomach revolted and he vomited. "I'm gettin' out," he gasped. "Christ, I'd rather die in the open." He heaved hideously, then the paroxysm passed. He was quiet for a few minutes, only his little eyes moving, darting from the window to the leader and back to the window, then up at the moon. As it vanished behind a small cloud he took a deep breath and hurled himself through the opening of the window. He rolled over in a practised way into a crouch by the wall. It was at that moment Gavin stepped into the open, and the cloud uncovered the moon. Scrap swung the tommy gun, firing a short burst at the sea. Gavin went down behind a heap of stones.

"Anyone comes near, and that's what 'e gets." He saw Gavin's head rising above the stones. "Stay where you are," he snarled. "Or Gawd 'elp me, mister, I'll blast yer 'ead orf."

"Don't be a bloody fool. Put that thing down."

"Come and get it, if you want it so bad."

Gavin got to his feet and moved forward very slowly.

"Get back, mister. I'm warnin' you."

"You're wanted for poaching deer," said Gavin, watching the little black muzzle as it jerked menacingly towards him. "But if you hit anyone with that thing, then you'll be wanted for something a good deal worse."

"Heh," shouted Mike from behind. "If there's anyone in the cottage, tell that trigger-happy little bastard to throw away his toy and put his hands up."

"If you shoot me, you'll hang," said Gavin. He was close enough to see the look on the man's face: hate and fear, the bared teeth of a cornered beast.

"Let me worry about that, mister. Just you keep your distance, that's all."

"Drop it. Go on." Gavin took another short step forward. With a vicious oath the man straightened up and ran.

And he ran straight for the Quaking Sands.

"Not that way. Stop!"

Gavin went after him, hearing Margaret's voice behind him.

"No, Gavin!"

The poacher stopped and spun round snarling. "Don't you come no nearer, mister. For the last time——" He jerked the tommy gun warningly. As he did so he retreated step by step, and every step took him closer to the fringes of the smooth white sands.

"For God's sake, man. Quicksands!"

"Stay where you are, Scrap," shouted the leader from the cottage. "Those are quicksands. You'll never get out, Jimmy says."

But the man paid no heed. Back, back he went, just as the wounded stag had edged into the Wailing Loch. By now he was in the outer fringes of the Sands and already he could feel the gentle tug at his feet. Hardly noticing, never taking his eyes from Gavin and, beyond him, Mike, he pulled his boots clear with a small effort and went backwards to meet the death that waited so patiently, gurgling softly beneath the beautiful moonlit Sands.

Then, as though eager to die, he turned and stumbled deeper into that terrible place. Still Gavin followed, keeping to the clumps of rushes. He could feel them, springy and deadly, trembling beneath his weight.

"Watch it, Gavin. Let him go if he wants to."

Gavin was deaf to Mike's advice and to Margaret crying, "Please come back." He called on the man to stop before it was too late. The moon vanished. He stopped, swaying perilously on two clumps. Ahead he could hear sudden panting fear in the darkness; the clattering thump as the tommy gun landed in the Sands.

"Christ, I'm sinking. I'm going down."

Gavin heard frantic, gasping struggles..

"Keep still. Don't struggle. For God's sake, keep still."

"But I'm being sucked down. They're pulling me under. Get me out, mister. Jesus, help me. Get me out!" The voice was shrill and breaking with fear. And in the cold eye of the moon Gavin saw the terror livid on the man's face. The Sands were half-way up to his knees, clasping his legs ever more tightly so that now he could no longer turn towards safety but could only scream for mercy from the Sands themselves. He heaved frenziedly at his legs, twisting his body this way, that way, like a fly stuck in treacle. There was no sign of the weapon. Gavin poised himself, then jumped for a big clump just behind the man's arching back.

"Turn round. You've *got* to turn round. It's your only chance. Quickly, before you're any deeper. Go on, man, you can do it." He dared not touch the man. If one of the wildly flailing arms were to knock him off the clump that would be the finish; they'd both go under.

"Well done. Come on. Now the other leg. That's it. You've done it."

The man was round, facing him. His eyes were bulging from his head and the breath whistled from his gaping mouth.

Gavin tore off his jacket and flung it in front of the man.

"Here—take this." Mike passed him Margaret's sheepskin coat from behind. Gavin threw that down.

"Lean forward," he ordered.

But the man was too mad with fear. All he did was to scream. "Save me! Suffering Jesus, save me. I'm going under. I'll suffocate. Christ Almighty, I'll suffocate."

"Shut up!" snapped Gavin. "Shut up and listen to me. You've got to lean forward. Throw yourself on those coats. LISTEN TO ME! In a moment you'll be up to your thighs, then your waist. Then you've had it. Nothing'll get you out. D'you understand? Nothing on God's earth'll get you out. Forward, man, forward!"

The Quaking Sands were never in a hurry. They had all the time in the world in which to swallow their victims. A man would have ample time for fear as he went down. Even at the very last he would have quite a few terrible seconds to stare at the cold calm beauty of the starlit sky directly above him as he thrust his head back, keeping his nostrils clear of the soft wet sand that was closing across his face for ever. Oh, yes, a man sinking slowly to his death in the Sands would have long moments for anticipation and repentance.

Below him Gavin could hear the dreadful sounds of the Sands stirred to slow sluggish excitement by the struggles of their victim. The man arched himself back, then forward, like a cut worm. He went on screaming: at God, at Jesus, at Gavin, to save him, not to let him be buried alive.

Gavin and Mike lay down with their weight supported by the clumps of rushes. They each stretched out an arm, and each grabbed a clawing hand. The leader of the poachers had run from the cottage with a broken tabletop. They slid it forward on the coats and pulled. They pulled till the sweat blinded their eyes and their hearts bumped and pounded like trip hammers, and very, very slowly, inch by inch, they defeated the stubborn Sands and drew the wretched man to safety. They dragged him back from a disgusting and degrading death and back on to solid ground where they collapsed utterly spent, with Scrap, who had hoped to make some easy money killing a few deer, sprawled half conscious between them.

"If he'd gone another couple of inches," said Mike, getting to his feet, brushing the sand and snow off himself, "we'd never have got him out."

"I suppose I should thank you for saving his fairly worthless life," said the leader of the poachers, running his hand through his thick blond hair.

Mike glanced at him without speaking, then he spat on the ground.

[12]

THEY collected driftwood and bits of boarding from the cottage and built a fire in the shelter of a broken wall. They did what they could for Robertson, splinting his leg with wood, filling him with whisky from Mike's bottomless flask and placing him beneath a pile of coats near the heat of the leaping flames. The little man, Scrap, sat silently with his head bowed between his upraised knees, never looking up. Mike smoked his pipe, stirring the edges of the fire with his golf club so that sparks shot high into the moonlight. Now and then he threw a quick angry glance at the blond man who lay propped on his elbow, seemingly unperturbed. Beyond the blaze Gavin stood with his back to the wall. Margaret sat at his feet, holding her hands to the blaze. The sky was clear but the wind came over the wall, flattening the tops of the tall flames and whirling away the sparks.

Gavin stooped for the spotlight he had discovered in the cottage. For the third time he pointed the beam up the glen and signalled, short-long, short-long.

"One of them ought to see it." It was not going to be easy to get Robertson back to the road, and they would need assistance. They had broken down what was left of the cottage door; that would have to do for a stretcher.

"Surely we can manage," said Margaret. The sooner they got the man to hospital the better. "After all, there are five of us and it's bright moonlight."

"Not yet," said Mike quietly. "There's a little matter to settle first."

"But——"

"Sorry, Margaret. He'll just have to wait." She had never heard him speak like that before. Very quiet, very firm; all his heartiness stripped away, leaving a much older man. She looked at his face. And a much harder man. He turned to the blond man.

"Why did you do it?" he asked, still very quiet.

There was a long pause, then the man answered coolly: "Don't you ever get bored with your life? Don't you ever want excitement, adventure, whatever you like to call it? Something to make the time pass quicker?"

"And so you decided to go in for deer poaching," Gavin said. "Adventure without much risk," he added scornfully.

"There's the challenge of the thing." The man's easy smile gleamed in the firelight.

"Challenge? Where the hell's the challenge? Slaughtering animals haphazard with tommy guns and risking a possible fine of a few quid." Mike snorted.

Robertson stifled a groan, twisting his head from side to side. Margaret went over to him; she wiped his forehead and lips with her handkerchief.

"We must get him back," she said.

"It's only a broken leg," said Mike in that same hard voice. "He'll live." He threw across the flask. "Give him another pull."

The spirits dribbled from the corner of the slack mouth as Robertson nodded his gratitude, then his eyes closed and he lay back.

"How many of you are there?" Gavin asked.

"Counting myself, four. Kindred spirits, you might say." He smiled at Margaret.

"You think it's all a bloody good joke, don't you?" Mike threw on another lump of wood.

"What isn't?"

Margaret whirled on him. "Killing and wounding. Inflicting pain and suffering to make the time pass quicker. If this is your idea of adventure, fun, then—well, God help you, that's all I can say."

Gavin looked at his wife with the admiration he so often felt; at the rounded shadows of her small breasts rising and falling quickly below the soft blue jersey; at her fire-flushed, scornful little face. For the first time the blond man seemed shaken out of his calm. He averted his gaze and did not answer.

"The lady's speaking to you," said Mike.

"You come here," she went on, "with your beastly guns and kill our deer and——"

The man looked up.

"*Your* deer?"

"Yes," she said. "Our deer. They belong here, this is their home, and it's our home too. We love it as we love the deer. But I don't suppose you'd understand anything like that." Her mouth curled in disgust.

He inclined his head in a little mock bow. "You're making me feel terribly ashamed." He smiled his charming smile.

"Cut it out," growled Mike. "You'll be feeling a ruddy sight more than ashamed by the time we've done with you." The man gave a careless little shrug that said, just as you like, it's all the same to me.

"Where d'you come from?" Gavin asked.

"Actually my home's in London. Eaton Place. You may know it." He spoke in a light social voice as much as to say, You and I are equals. We can speak the same civilised, cultured language. You and I can sort out this silly little misunderstanding like gentlemen. Surely there's no need for unpleasantness. Not between men of the world. Over a glass of port, my dear chap, over a glass of port. "But for the last two or three months I've been staying at my country place. In case you're curious, nowhere near here. Very handy though, and really quite comfortable. Nothing pretentious of course, just a farmhouse. But quite adequate for our simple needs." He sighed. "Until we came here, we'd done not too badly at all. Covered our expenses nicely. To be quite frank, I'd expected to make our profit over here, but—ah, well, what you gain on the swings——"

"And *he* showed you where to go," said Gavin, nodding at Robertson.

"For a consideration, yes. Look here," he went on, "why don't we call it quits? It's a fair cop, as they say. We've had a good run for our money and now you've got us." He shrugged again.

"And what sort of a run did the deer have?" Margaret's eyes regarded him as though he was some obnoxious, crawling thing.

"I am terribly sorry to have upset you"—another little bow. "If I'd had any idea how you'd feel——"

"You'd have gone to some other place where everyone was too bloody wet to try and stop you," broke in Mike.

"It certainly might have been more satisfactory, yes."

"Well, you didn't. You came here. And now, by God, you're going to pay for it." Mike jabbed fiercely at the fire with the golf club.

"Surely we can settle this business between ourselves, without actually getting involved with the police." He paused, looking at each of them in turn. No one spoke. "Tell you what, supposing I was to pay for any inconvenience suffered? Petrol used, sleep lost, that sort of thing."

No answer.

"I'll give you my word we shan't come back. My dear chap, I can take a hint as well as the next man, and I can see the natives are not exactly tumbling over themselves to make us welcome. What do you say? After all, these two have had a pretty rough time of it." He indicated the other two poachers. Still no one spoke.

"You know as well as I do it's a sheer waste of time prosecuting. Even if they do find us guilty, which I very much doubt, what'll we get? At the very most a fiver each. It's not worth the candle, it really isn't. Not just for a few deer."

"Aren't you forgetting one or two things?"

The man stared at Gavin.

"Am I?"

"Shooting with intent to kill on"—Gavin counted on his fingers—"at least four separate occasions." Scrap raised his head slightly.

"You'd never prove it, not in a month of Sundays."

"No?"

"The only shots we fired were at deer."

"The police think otherwise."

"Let them. What good's that in court?"

"Two dead rams," said Gavin bleakly. "Not to mention an attempt to sink our boat."

"Rams? Boat? My dear chap, you have the advantage of me."

"Are you trying to tell us you know nothing about it? What about the man who landed at Glenaila this afternoon—the one who's with Constable McPhail at the moment."

"Search me." His ignorance was beautifully simulated.

Mike jumped to his feet. "There's been enough ruddy talk. Now I'll tell you what's going to be done. You want to settle this business among ourselves. Right, so do I." He towered, large and menacing, over the other man. Scrap looked up for the first time. Robertson opened his eyes. A gust of wind swooped low over the fire, scattering the flames.

"I'll tell you why." Mike spoke very slowly and very distinctly. "First, because it's a ruddy waste of time handing you over. And second——" he paused. "Secondly, because I'm going to belt the daylights out of you. Get up!" But the man did not move. Margaret went round the fire to Gavin. Scrap stared with dull, frightened eyes.

"Come on. Get up!"

"Suppose I don't?"

"I'll give you till I count five, then I'll start on you where you are. One—two——"

"No, Mike," cried Margaret. "You can't."

"Sorry, Margaret."

Gavin took her hand.

"Three——"

"This is childish," said the man sullenly.

"Four——"

"I could have you up for assault. I suppose you know that."

"Try it. Five."

The man was on his feet, quick and lithe as a cat. "All right, if that's the way you want it."

"You're damned right, that's the way I want it."

"Stay here," Gavin told Margaret. He picked up the rifle. "Look after Robertson. Come on, you." He nodded at Scrap.

"But, Gavin——"

"He's right, love. It's the only way. Think of the deer. Think of Simon and Peter."

"I know, darling, but this—this seems so—so——"

"Can you think of a better answer?"

* * * * *

They fought beyond the firelight beneath the cold eye of the moon; on an open stretch of grass patched with snow, between the wall and the sea. The great white mountains looked down on them and flecks of spray from the crashing surf flicked across their grim faces. It was a fitting place for violence. Gulls, mewing mournfully, floated on the wind above the fighters, surprised by these strange, circling creatures.

They moved round each other warily two or three times, then the blond man darted close, stabbing at Mike's face, one-two-three, very fast on his feet, knowing how to use his fists. Mike shook his head in surprise, and blood began to trickle from his nose, slowly turning his scrubby moustache to a wet red growth. His opponent grinned.

"Well," he taunted, "I thought you were going to tear me

apart." He danced on his toes, kicking up a little spray of snow. He skipped back from a powerful left swing that grazed his forehead, ducked expertly below a right that would have finished the fight, and smashed his fist hard on the bleeding nose. Gavin watched anxiously. Mike seemed slow, almost cumbersome beside the smaller man. Scrap stood with his hands in his pockets stamping his feet up and down, showing little interest in what was going on. But his eyes flickered briefly as the blond man beat another quick tattoo of blows on Mike's ribs, jumped back, his teeth bared in a panting grin.

"Come on, Mike. For God's sake!"

"Yes," echoed the blond man mockingly. "Come on. What are you waiting for?"

This time it was Mike who attacked, feinting twice for the head. The man's hands came up instinctively, leaving his body wide open. Gavin heard the gasping grunt as Mike's fist buried itself deep in his stomach. The man doubled up, and as he did so an uppercut slammed into his face. For a few seconds he staggered about groggily, sucking at the air like a stranded fish, clutching at his stomach. Mike watched him, keeping very close. The man certainly had his share of courage. Fighting desperately for breath he came at the big man, his arms pawing weakly.

Mike met the feeble attack with a left that stopped the blond man in his tracks; his right crashed home full on the other's mouth. He swung again, landing high on the cheekbone, then with all his strength and weight at the jaw. The noise of the blow was sickening. The pale-blue eyes went glassy, the hands dropped, the knees began to buckle. Mike hit him again, twice more as he went down. The blond man rolled slowly on to his face and lay still, the blood from his shattered mouth staining the snow.

Mike stood over him, breathing heavily.

"That's for the deer you left to die," he snarled. "Get up, you bastard, get up and take what's coming to you."

Gavin put a restraining hand on his arm. "No, Mike, that's enough. You don't have to kill him."

Mike shook his head and drew the back of his hand across his mouth. He swung round on Scrap.

"If you come back, so help me, I'll kill you and throw you back into those ruddy sands. Get it? Answer me, you dirty little swine." He raised his fist and the man cringed away.

"By God, I'll teach you to shoot at people. Not so funny when you haven't a ruddy gun in your hand, is it?" Mike hit him. The man squealed with pain and terror. Mike hit him again. This time he dropped.

"Pass this round among your pals. Spread it about." Scrap sat up, nursing his left eye. "You're bloody lucky we don't beat you up good and proper."

They hauled the blond man to his feet and took him back to the fire, trailing him between them like a straw dummy. Gavin filled Robertson's cap from the burn. The shock of the cold water brought the blond man round. Margaret bathed his bruised, battered face. His eyes were slits in the swollen purple flesh and his lips were red rubber; he had lost three of his front teeth. Gavin could see she was shocked, but she did not say anything.

"Here," said Mike, removing his camouflage jacket, "put this on." The man was shivering, but something approaching a smile twisted the ruin of his mouth.

"You must think a lot of your deer," he said thickly.

"Yes," said Margaret, "we do. Now keep still and I'll try and do something to that cheek."

Before leaving, Gavin took the rifle and threw it far into the Quaking Sands.

"That's that," he said.

As gently as they could they placed Robertson on the broken door, then they started on the slow journey back up the glen, with Mike in the lead, mopping his nose; then the two poachers stumbling slowly along with the injured man;

Gavin and Margaret at the back. Frequently they had to stop. After a while Mike and Gavin took over.

At the stepping-stones they were met by John Grant.

"What luck, Mr Blair?"

"We got them. And you?"

"We were finding the vehicles all right. A van and a great ugly thing of a shooting brake—man alive, but what's that?" The stalker stooped close to Robertson.

"Well, well, so it's Jimmy Robertson. Man, but he sounds very sick." They lowered the door to the ground.

"Broke his leg."

"Och, well, Captain, maybe that'll be keeping him out of any more mischief." He peered at the other two. "They are looking very sick too. Good Lord above, but this fellow has surely been falling on his face. I was nearly forgetting that the Inspector of Police is waiting on the road. He has Donald with him."

"The Inspector?" Gavin looked at Mike.

"Aye, himself. And not pleased at all, the wee fellow. Not with himself, nor with anyone else. Stamping about like an angry bee he is. And them arriving"—his teeth gleamed in his beard—"just as Kenny was explaining to the poaching rascal at the vehicles he should not have been trying to run away." A short laugh rumbled in his throat. "He is a handy one with his hands is Kenny Carmichael. There was another of the little devils who was falling on his face."

With considerable difficulty they carried the injured man across the slippery stones. A rising wind helped them on their way up the last winding climb out of the glen, and by the time they reached the road fresh snow was falling.

Inspector Marr was marching up and down by himself, keeping warm. As John had said, he was not pleased with life. Even though it looked as if they'd really got the poachers, vehicles, everything. But the way it had been done, the trouble there'd be. He groaned inwardly as he marched. Fools! Blasted hot-headed fools! He turned up the collar of his overcoat against the shower. He wondered what the devil had been going on, how much longer he would have to hang about. Snow went down his neck. If only that damned telephone hadn't been so bad, he'd have got out here in time to take charge and stop all this amateur mucking about. Taking the law into their own hands. Anarchy, that's what it could lead to, this sort of thing, just plain blasted anarchy. People shooting at each other. Someone might be lying out there at the moment with a bullet through his guts. He groaned again at the very thought. God's sakes there'd be hell to pay! And if the papers got hold of it—ye gods! Yet somebody had to stop these men, somehow. Desperate times, desperate measures. God's sakes, who'd be a policeman? He thought of Kenny's bland face and innocent voice and the poacher sitting in the police car with an eye like a damned squashed tomato.

"Well now, Inspector, I'm thinking he must have been running into the corner of the van here."

Torches were shining through the snow; he saw figures moving.

"That you, Inspector?"

"Yes." He saw the shape on the ground and his heart sank.

"Here they are, three of them."

"Sorry we couldn't wait for you," boomed Mike. The Inspector shone his torch on Robertson.

"It's his leg," said Margaret. "It's very badly broken. He must get to hospital as soon as possible." Marr looked up, surprised.

"My wife," said Gavin. "Inspector Marr." Marr nodded politely. Ye gods, so they even take their wives along. He allowed the beam of his torch to play slowly across the assembled faces.

"Strewth, what happened to him?"

The blond man winced away from the bright light.

Donald let out a long whistle of astonishment. "He looks as if he ran into a door."

"He did," said Mike flatly.

"And what about you? Same door?"

Mike's nose was bleeding again; one eye was darkly ringed. "That's right."

Marr rose to his feet. So that's how it was going to be. Bloody fools.

"Get him into the van. Farquhar!"

"Yessir."

"Take this man to the hospital. Then go back to the Station."

"Very good, sir."

"Tell them——" he paused.

"I think he's been drinking," volunteered Mike quite truthfully, looking up at a starlit gap in the snow clouds.

"Maybe he was falling over a pile of stones or——"

"All right, that'll do," snapped Marr.

They put Robertson into the back of the van. Marr took the driver aside for a moment.

"Well, John," said Donald, "so you were not listening to what I was telling you." He shook his head sorrowfully.

"No, Donald, I'm afraid we were not."

Marr came striding back. "I don't know what the devil's been going on tonight, but I mean to find out." He went up to Gavin, thrust his face close in the darkness.

"I told you once, the law takes a poor view of people getting hurt, even if they deserve it. Remember?"

"Yes, I remember."

"Well then, why the devil couldn't you have left this to us?"

"For the very simple reason, you weren't here," said Margaret. "Now, couldn't we continue this somewhere warmer? It's awfully cold standing here."

"What should we be doing with these fellows?" The stalker

jabbed his pipe-stem at the shivering, melancholy figures of the poachers.

"I think it might be best if you two gentlemen were to avail yourselves of the hospitality of the Station," said the Inspector bleakly. Scrap began to protest, but the blond man silenced him.

"He's right," he muttered painfully from his broken mouth.

"I'm glad you see it that way. At the Station you can have attention for your injuries and the privacy you wouldn't find if you were to go to a hotel at this time of night. And I'm sure you'll agree, gentlemen, that under the circumstances privacy and quietness will be welcome. Then in the morning we shall see what's to be done. Right, get them into the car, Donald." He swung round on the others.

"I'll want to see you tomorrow. All of you."

The stalker removed his pipe and spat.

"So that's all the ruddy thanks we get," growled Mike angrily.

Fortunately, before things could get more unpleasant a thick squall swept among them and they had to turn their faces from the swirling, stinging snow.

* * * * *

The next afternoon Inspector Marr stood before the fire in the living-room of Glenaila, dressed in his baggy old suit but wearing a purposeful look on his good-natured face. There had been quite a long silence while the others waited for him to speak, broken by the heavy patter of rain on the windows and the occasional little hiss of drops in the fire. Outside, the snow which had fallen during the night was being fast washed away down the cloud-covered hills. It was a raw and sodden day. Water gurgled in the gutters as the four of them waited for what the Inspector had to say. Gavin perched beside his wife on the arm of her chair. Mike and John sat side by side, twin giants on the sagging sofa.

"Now," said Marr briskly, "I'd like to know exactly what did happen last night!" No one answered. He allowed his sharp glance to dart from one to the other. Gavin looked at Mike; the stalker fiddled with his watch-chain, gazing down at his huge boots.

"I think you'd better, Gavin," said Margaret.

Mike murmured encouragement. Gavin met the Inspector's bland gaze. "As you know," he said, "last night the poachers came back." He paused. "And this time we were lucky enough to catch them. That's about all there is to it, Inspector. You probably know as much about it as we do."

"And now they're all yours," added Mike.

"From the beginning, please," insisted Marr quietly. "The full story—if you don't mind." His lips shut in a tight little smile. "From when the boat came into the bay here." He looked out to where the 'Sea Parrot' rode the swell, just visible through the curtains of rain.

"Well, John and I were out after a hummel on Beinn Gobhair when we first saw the boat. . . ." Marr swayed backwards and forwards on his toes, listening intently, now and then asking a question, now and then nodding his head. He pulled continually at his moustache.

"At Hump Bridge we dropped off the others and——"

"The others?"

"Mike. Kenny. And John to go down the Black Burn."

"I see. Perhaps, Mr Grant, you would be good enough to carry on from here."

The stalker took time to marshal his thoughts and turn them into slow lilting words. At one point Marr broke in.

"You say this man shouted at you before he fired?"

"Aye, he did. Something about 'Here is one to be taking home with you'. He was firing twice. Tracer bullets. The first one was missing me by—och, I'm telling you, by a foot maybe. No more."

"And then?"

"And then I was chasing the little devils and if it hadn't been for the pain in my back I'd have been catching them right enough."

"But they got away?"

"Aye, they were getting away in a shower of snow."

"What did you do then, Mr Grant?"

"I was joined by the Captain here. Him and Kenny Carmichael."

"I see. Would you care to continue, Captain Downie?"

"As soon as the shooting started we came down off Creag Dhu fast as we could. On the way Kenny was damn nearly hit by a tracer. Ruddy ricochet, by the sound of it. Well, anyway, we joined up with John and had a bit of a chinwag over what to do. To cut a long story, etcetera, I went on down the glen and the other two nipped back to scupper the transport. That's where you met 'em. I got as far as the entrance to the Chasm where I met up with the Blairs. We pushed on till we got to the sea, had a scout around but couldn't spot anything till we saw this ruddy cap lying by the cottage. So we knew we'd got the brutes then and I said——"

Marr held up a restraining hand. "Thank you, Captain," he said with a smile. "A masterly account. Now, Mr Blair, could we hear from you what happened then?"

Gavin continued the story until the moment when Scrap had jumped from the window, then he paused.

"Well, Mr Blair?"

"He loosed off a short burst from the tommy gun. No, I don't think it was *at* anyone, just to discourage us from coming too close, I suppose, then he got up and ran." He paused again. The Inspector waited, with his eyebrows slightly raised.

"Perhaps you remember what happened, Mrs Blair?"

"Yes," she answered firmly. "I do. The man ran straight into the Quaking Sands, they're quicksands, and my husband ran after him——"

"Yes," Mike burst out. "And risked his ruddy life. Good

grief, Inspector, he ought to get a ruddy medal for what he did last night instead of being asked a lot of damn-fool questions."

"Steady on, Mike," said Gavin. "The Inspector's only doing his job."

"I just want it on the record, old boy, that's all."

"For your information, Captain, it is already on the record. The man realises he owes his life to Mr Blair." Marr's voice was cold. "For your further information, part of my job happens to be asking damn-fool questions." He looked at them squarely, each in turn, frowning. "Now listen to me," he snapped. "All of you."

There was an edge to his tone they had never heard before. "I want one point clearly understood. The law does not, and *will* not tolerate violence of any sort, however much"—he held up his hand—"Please allow me to finish, Captain Downie—however much it may seem to be justified at the time." His gaze settled firmly on Mike.

"On this particular occasion you have got away with it. You've achieved your object."

"But surely it was your object too?" Margaret said.

"That is beside the point, Mrs Blair. A policeman's duty is to uphold the law and, as I have already pointed out, I am a policeman. Please remember that." The hardness faded slightly. "Whatever any of us personally feels about the victim who fights back—and, believe me, we very often sympathise most strongly—we cannot allow our feelings to influence our actions."

"Yes, Inspector, we all realise that. But surely in a case like this you don't"—Mike floundered—"well, dammit man, you're not going to get unpleasant over something that ought to have been done ages ago. Good grief, we've cleaned out the ruddy sewer for you. You ought to be grateful. Think of all the bumph-work we've saved you."

The Inspector's frown thawed to the suspicion of a smile.

"Next time—should there be a next time," he answered, "for God's sake come to us. Or there'll be trouble. Really serious trouble. And a great deal of bumph-work for all of us."

"But we did, Inspector, we kept on coming to you. But nothing seemed to happen." Margaret smiled sweetly, regarding him from beneath her dark eyelashes.

"So you decided to take the law into your own hands, Mrs Blair." He smiled inwardly at the size of her hands, and continued:

"You decided to teach these men a lesson, was that it?"

"Aye," interrupted the stalker. "Aye, that was it right enough. A lesson they would not be forgetting in a hurry. Someone had to be showing the wicked rascals they could not be getting away with their dirty little game."

"And in your opinion the best answer was to beat them up?"

"Heh!" exploded Mike. "Less of the beating-up, Inspector. It was a perfectly fair fight." He touched his eye. "Let's get something else straight for the record. The scrap was entirely my idea. If anyone's for the high jump then it's Joe Soap Downie. No one else."

"Very noble," said the Inspector dryly. "But I'm not interested in Sydney Carton confessions. Besides, our friends have decided, very wisely under the circumstances—and I may add, very fortunately for certain of us present—to say nothing about the—ah—state of their health."

Mike threw back his head and roared.

"Let me remind you, Captain, it's not really a laughing matter."

"Oh, come off it, Inspector. State of health!" He chuckled away to himself.

Marr waited patiently. "I don't think you quite understand," he said very seriously. "If either of those men had decided to press a charge of assault the consequences might well have been very unpleasant. Very unpleasant indeed."

"Assault?" Margaret sat bolt upright, eyes round with astonishment.

"Yes, Mrs Blair, assault."

"But how on earth could they possibly charge us with anything? After what they've done here." Deep rumbles of agreement from the stalker. "They've poached our deer in the most horrible way. They've shot at us, they've even tried to sink our boat——"

"What about the rams?" Gavin said.

"Yes," she flared. "What about Simon and Peter?"

Marr looked at her in silence. Anger suited her, he thought. He knew she was right; he knew they were all right. He also knew in his heart of hearts that in their position he would very likely have done the same. So would anyone with any guts and spirit who felt as strongly about the land and the animals as these people did. Inspector Marr wished that as a policeman he didn't find himself quite so often on the wrong side of the fence. He pulled himself together with an effort.

"Mrs Blair," he said quietly. "We all know they were in the Forest to poach deer, this time and on the previous occasions. We have your word for it that you were shot at more than once, and having seen those men I have no reason to doubt the fact. As well as this, two of your rams had their throats cut. Yes, and the business of the boat. Right then, on the face of it you have plenty to go on——" he paused. "But in fact, and in court, you have absolutely nothing."

"But they *did* it," she cried. "We know they did it."

"You may know. *I* may know. Everyone in the whole place may know, but that is not proof."

Gavin saw the mutinous expression on her flushed face. "He's right, Margaret." Then he smiled. "Presumably the same applies from our point of view," he said.

Marr looked puzzled.

"We know how the poachers got into such a poor state of

health. They know. *You* know. Everyone in the whole place may know. But that of course is not proof, is it, Inspector?"

"Well put, old boy." Mike thumped his chair.

Marr grinned.

"Exactly. Now, if you'll accept some fairly unofficial advice, I suggest we forget last night. Our friends have already left the district." He studied his nails. "I persuaded them they might possibly find it preferable to leave quietly with the minimum of fuss and to-do. Just between you and me and that splendid little calf over there, I think they might well have been less co-operative if you hadn't pulled that rather disagreeable man out of the quicksands. However, be that as it may, they've gone. And something tells me they're unlikely to come back. With any luck the word will get round that Bealtuinn is a spot to be avoided. Unofficially, you've done a damn good job. Officially, don't ever try it again."

"What about you, Inspector? I mean, you won't get into trouble, will you, because of us or anything?"

"No, Mrs Blair, I don't think so." He laughed. "My conscience is quite clear, and so, I hope, is my report. Let's leave it at that, shall we?"

"Can you be telling us about Jimmy Robertson?"

"Yes, Mr Grant. You'll be pleased to hear he had a comfortable night and is now resting in a hospital bed after his very—ah—sad accident. A pretty nasty break, I believe." Another brief smile touched his lips. "It seems he must have fallen off his bicycle. On his way home early last night as far as we could gather, during one of those thick showers. Some ditch or other." He returned to the careful study of his nails. Margaret spoke first.

"Inspector, you're wonderful," she said warmly.

Mike slapped his leg. "Good grief, I've got to hand it to you all right. Sad accident!" He bellowed with laughter.

"Well, well," observed Grant slowly. "Maybe the police are not the half-baked fellows I was sometimes thinking them."

"Thank you," said Marr. He stretched, rubbed his hands together and let out a long heart-felt sigh.

"And that, I hope, is that," he said.

"You'll stay and have some tea. Do."

"Good grief, Maggie, surely he's worth something stronger than tea." Light laughter all round, during which Chiquita left her basket and trotted across to Margaret, tinkling her bell and shaking her head. On the way she allowed Marr to stroke her back.

"She likes you," smiled Margaret, caressing the velvet ears.

"Aye, she's knowing whose side you're on right enough."

The calf glowed rich chestnut-red in the firelight. Already it was growing dark outside, and the rain still pelted down. The Inspector could not stay for tea. John Grant consulted his turnip watch. Thank you, Mrs Blair, but he would have to be getting back.

They stood in the porch, Margaret and Gavin and Mike, to watch the others leave.

"Come back again soon, won't you, Inspector?" she called through the rain.

"I will." How nice it would be, he found himself thinking as he drove away, if one day she was to call me by my Christian name.

"Good bloke that. Ruddy good bloke."

"Yes," said Gavin. "He is."

"Well, Mr Blair, we'll not be forgetting what you and Mrs Blair have done for Bealtuinn."

"Nonsense, John. It was just as much you. And you, Mike."

"And Kenny," added Margaret.

"Not forgetting the stone-slinging Minister."

"And poor Donald who'd have done every sort of thing if he'd ever been at the right place at the right time."

"In fact," she said, "it was all of us."

"Combined op, Maggie."

She held her hand under the water dripping off the porch.

"Ugh, what a night."

"But the deer are safe," Gavin said.

"Aye, Mr Blair, the deer are safe right enough." John Grant's old car splashed away through the pouring dusk.

Pusan opened a sleepy eye as they came back to the fire. The calf lay with her head on his flank, staring into the flames. Her bell tinkled as she turned to look at Margaret, then she lowered her head and slept. Gavin pulled the curtains against the rain battering at the windows, and lit the purring lamps.

"You'll stay the night," he said.

"Well, I——"

"Of course you will, Mike," Margaret insisted.

"Tonight," said Gavin firmly. "We are going to celebrate."

EPILOGUE

SPRING had come to Bealtuinn, that lonely peaceful corner of land jutting into the Atlantic like the prow of a great ship. The last of the snows had melted from all but the highest northern faces of the mountains, and the sunshine was golden on the hills and bottle-green on the sea.

On the grey cliffs of Corridon the myriad seabirds had begun their noisy search for nesting space and the cock grouse crowed defiantly on the long slope of Beinn Bhreac. Rabbits played skittishly on the tender new grass round the ruined cottage and along the edges of the Quaking Sands. The wild swans had flown from Loch nan Eala, leaving the sands to the deer and the waters to the otters and the divers which came to nest. The iron had lifted from the ground and at last there was warmth in the April sun, and the sea breezes which bent the cotton grass and sighed softly round Glenaila no longer carried the knife-edge of winter. Gavin and Margaret sat in the afternoon sunshine on a grassy hillock by their little beach. Beside them lay Pusan asleep, with his scarred head rested on his white paws. Not far away, on the tide line, Chiquita poked about in the gleaming seaweed, now and then skipping hastily out of the way of the surging tide. The tawny green mountains patched with young bracken shimmered behind a slight heat-haze. Gavin put down his glass. He had been watching the sheep moving among the trees on Coraval. Soon, any day now, the ewes would begin to drop their lambs; then there would be no time for lazing in the sun. He lay back, his face upturned to the sun, relaxed and contented, enjoying the feel of Margaret's fingers in his hair. But he did not speak. Gulls mewed and cried above the slow sullen music of the sea as the great rollers came sweeping from the West to thunder in rainbow spray upon their shore.

"Darling," she said.

"Yes."

"There are lots of deer on the Big Sister. They look just like little points of flame."

Sleepily he rolled over on his elbow. Red-gold specks stood out on the broad green apron of grass, just below the receding snow line.

"You're very romantic today. Points of flame." He smiled.

"I feel romantic."

"They're going back to the tops," he said. "We won't be seeing them round the house any more. Not till next winter."

"We'll miss them, won't we?"

"Yes."

"But they won't be far away," she said.

"No, Margaret, they'll never be far away."

He looked fondly at his wife. Then he looked at their gay white house and beyond to the specks of their sheep dotted across the slopes of the bronze mountains; he looked back to the sea, at the 'Sea Parrot' nodding gently at her scarlet buoy. He watched the red-deer calf as she hopped from rock to rock with superb grace; he saw the white splinters of the gulls milling above the Knucklebones. He opened his mouth to speak but said nothing. Instead he plucked a length of grass and put it between his teeth, then placing one hand on his wife's small round arm and the other on Pusan's warm coat, Gavin Blair closed his eyes, utterly content.

Three miles away, below the Cave of the Laughing Men, the big black stag lay peacefully in the sheltered warmth, his jaws moved slowly with an easy unhurried rhythm, but his head hardly moved at all, for he was well guarded. His young companion grazed nearby and the little knobs of sprouting horn stood out proudly as he looked up every now and then from feeding. The soft white spots of extreme youth had almost vanished from his coat, but the scar of the bullet still showed as a puckered, hairless furrow across his back. His eyes were wary but untroubled, and his flaring wet nostrils picked up no scent of danger; satisfied, he returned to his grazing.

The black stag lowered his great head in the sunlight, closed his eyes and dozed, while the flies murmured lazily round his faintly twitching ears and a wheatear came to perch on a stone, bobbing up and down and fanning its tail. Curlew were calling in the distance, sad and tremulous, and for a moment the air vibrated with the sound of a green plover's slanting flight. The sigh of the breeze across the mountain was soothing as sleep itself.

Far above them a raven floated on still wings, alone in the blue afternoon, and the bird's keen eyes, ever on the watch for death, could see for many miles over the Forest of Bealtuinn. From the snow-cap of Beinn Mhor to the white line of surf in the Bay of the Splashing Seals. From the long crouching shape of Beinn Gobhair to the still, ebony waters of the Wailing Loch, the darting eyes looked out across a shining land softened by the coming of Spring .

The raven circled slowly, dragging the talons of its wings across the blue immensity of sky, uttering its strange cry, half bark, half bell. And the shadow of the bird swept backwards and forwards over the deer grazing on Creag Dhu, but they did not look up as they moved slowly into the soft sea breeze that came out of the West, from the very eye of the lowering molten sun.

THE END

[*See over*

AUTHOR'S NOTE

In April 1959, the Deer Bill (Scotland) was passed, incorporating, among many and varied clauses, stiffer penalties for deer poachers.

In practice, however, it appears that little or no difference has been made by the Deer Bill (Scotland).